Many Thanks for
all the Support
Bella

The Legacy of the Six Wolves

Hope you find much
in this story that
makes you smile...

Much love and
Best wishes

Alan Calder
Rawlney

The Legacy of the Six Wolves

Alan Calder Rawlings

Front Cover: 'The Green Boy'. Oil on canvas by Philip Rawlings

ISBN 978-1-84799-987-0

I would like to thank the following people for their help in the presentation of this book.

Caroline Denson, Kate Skillings, Ben Evans, Steve Gamblin and Jo MacNaughten

To Granddad

Wherever your soul, your conscience lies, be it plant, animal, human or just plain air, thanks for the love, the value and the encouragement you gave – your legacy is part of the forever.

Prologue

Cheriton village lay in a small shallow, a few miles from the busy throb of a dual carriageway from which veined various roads that encircled its breadth. Cheriton was a village that you could easily pass, its charm unseen. The narrow road that meandered through it witnessed a pleasing array of homes, some large, some small, some cloaked in creepers, whilst others nestled beneath the shade of aged trees. All in turn provided a home for an assortment of busy creatures that help make up the gamut of life.

From a hovering kestrel's eye, you could see its ornate leafy heart, from which spread the church, manor, hall, shop and the old school. To the north lay a small housing estate, to the west, fields. A weary farm lay in the south, while in the east stretched a rich, dense, ancient wood.

As does everything, Cheriton and its *life* was changing. Although some carried on regardless of the world's activities, others gave time to pause for necessary thought.

The season was summer and as the light faded from another working day, the moon surfaced, shimmering its pale nocturnal gaze upon the planet's surface.

Having tied her long red hair, which still looked radiant in her middle years, into a tidy bun and slipped into the comfort of a light nightdress, Judith Tench was almost ready for bed. All that was required now was for her mind to unwind. Judith's naked feet pattered across the kitchen tiles as she made for the brandy bottle sat upon the fridge, which had rattled loudly to a halt. Pouring a small glass, the familiar aroma of the brandy calmed Judith's nerves. Relaxed, she swung round to make for her reading chair, unaware of the looming shadow beyond the kitchen window that had dropped suddenly out of sight.

Having made herself comfortable, Judith slid her thumb between the pages of her book, which was marked with a tightly folded letter. Her eyes scanned down the narrative. On reaching the bottom she went to turn the page when the sound of the front door creaking open made her start.

'Livia, is that you?'

There was no response. She placed the letter deep within the book's cleavage and rising from her chair, stopped abruptly, shocked at the sight of a darkened figure standing within the depth of the living room door. Judith gave a light gasp before her eyes widened as if transfixed.

In the coolness of the night, the long uncut grass of Cheriton's fields whistled softly as its blades brushed one upon the other. The sudden rustle of approaching feet plunging through its mass made two resting larks spring from their cover, their loud shrieks and fretful wings failing to startle Judith Tench from her numb-like gaze, for she seemed to be drawn, drawn by some mysterious force. Onward her lonely figure travelled, until she reached the edge of Great Cheriton Wood.

The dark imposing wood with its fringe of hand-like leafy branches could just be seen. Beyond, the light was eventually swallowed to black. Only the occasional shots of soundless lightening lit the way now.

Unmoved, Judith walked towards the outskirts, where stood an old mossy gate. Without fixing her eyes, her hands felt down its post until her fingers identified the loose chain that held it. Slipping the restricting buckle through its loop, she allowed it to fall with a clang. The gate swung silently open and Judith entered the woodland's girth. Staring forward, she stepped between the lofty trees, beyond which, deep within, a strange hypnotic light seemed to emerge. Beneath the woodland's gapping, shadowy veil, Judith Tench disappeared.

Chapter 1

The Calling

Across the remote moors, another gunshot broke.
'Don't be a fool man,' bawled a policeman, dropping to his stomach. 'Give yourself up while there's still a chance.'

The policeman and his colleague grappled with the grass while peering at the fleeing figure below. They threw their heads down as again more gunshots broke, followed by a desperate scream. Anxious, they looked up.

The man had staggered into a treacherous mire, its mouth rapidly seizing him.

'No,' he screamed, horrified. But it was too late. The mud was oozing swiftly over his waist. Within moments it had crept up to his face. His eyes bulged with terror.

The shocked policemen hurried towards the bog's edge to witness the man's untimely end as he sank within the recesses of the bottomless earth.

'He'll be back,' uttered one of them.

An orchestration of music broke out and the film's credits rolled up the television screen, sending a thin light dancing around the Phillips' living room. William rolled onto his back and stretched out over the hard worn carpet. His hand searched for the remote control. Finding it, he aimed with precision at the screen and it instantly fizzed blank.

For a moment the old farmhouse fell still, its uneven ceilings, floors and walls resting in the dimness like some great motherly creature settled into sleep. William loved this time. He loved the reflective calm of night, knowing that his sister and parents, along with much of the country where now cosily tucked up in bed. It gave him a sense of excitement, for this was a young man who liked the dark, the otherworldly, the unknown.

Adjusting his hazel eyes, he followed a sphere of light thrown from the almost drawn curtains. It had landed on a photograph of his Granddad Jack. William had lovingly framed him in bark taken from an old oak deep within Great Cheriton wood, a regular haunt. As William smiled at the photo, he felt a wave of grief creep over his heart.

'Goodnight Granddad Jack me old mate,' he whispered, 'I miss you.'

Drawing himself from the floor he made toward the door and almost tumbled over the arm of an unseen chair. He turned to face the curtains. The sparse light was enough to offer bearings. He was about to reach for the door when an intense thud seemed to push unexpectedly at the window, its alarming sound arresting him with shock. William had never heard anything like it before. It was odd. Twisting round, he wondered what it could have been, finally reassuring himself that a sharp gust of wind had merely hit the glass.

He continued his silent search, but another strange blow gripped him again - the unmistakable sound of heavy breathing seeming to resonate from beyond. A shiver tingled across William's neck. His head faced the window stiffly as the breathing grew more rapid. Someone or something was outside. William wanted to find out what. While raising his hands, he stepped toward the curtains, his trembling fingers guessing the parting from which the thin light appeared to brighten. As he touched the soft fabric the breathing grew more rapid, suddenly braking into a heavy pant. Summoning his courage, William tore the curtains wide, but beyond was nothing, only the familiar twilight of the back garden, tinged blue by the moon's glow. For a moment he froze in the silence, before sighing with relief and closing the curtains firm.

Prior to venturing up the stairs, he paused to reflect. There *was* something outside, wasn't there? Scratching his arm he shivered at the thought. The farmhouse often made strange weary sounds, especially at night. Sometimes William saw and heard things and couldn't tell if it was simply his imagination or that he truly had a sense that others didn't.

Treading on known steps that would not creak meanly and give his game away, William eventually reached the landing, skilfully swinging round the banister in readiness to step toward his bedroom. Suddenly a creaking sound shot from his side, spilling light over his cowering body. His mother Jackie had crept out of the bathroom.

'William you terror!' she gasped, pulling her dressing gown about her. 'I might have known you'd be up watching those silly old movies.'

'Sorry,' he shrugged. 'I just couldn't resist. The hound from hell wouldn't have kept me back...I would have taken a biscuit.'

His mother, a dreamy, warm faced woman gave him a shrewd glance.

'Well, what with the cleaning monster arriving early tomorrow you can forget about a lie-in.'

William knew his granny, armed with duster, would head straight for 'the dungeon,' which she had aptly named his room.

'You can tell granny if she as much as steps past my threshold she'll find herself getting a good flogging.'

His mother stifled a smile.

'Come on now, to bed with you. We don't want to go waking the others. Your sister will think we're throwing a late night shindig.'

William frowned at the mention of his sister possibly awaking. He watched his mother tiptoe across the landing.

'Oh, mum. By the way,' he whispered, 'you didn't by any chance hear any strange sounds outside just now, did you?'

Intrigued, she turned.

'No...like what?'

'Breathing,' suggested William.

His mother gave a smirk.

'Perhaps your granny is right. These late night horrors are not healthy for a sensitive mind.' She tilted her head teasingly. 'Would you like the landing light left on my dear? After all, one is never too old to be frightened of the dark.'

William pulled an obviously dumb face.

'And on that note,' she concluded with a mock, wicked stare, 'goodnight.'

They both entered their rooms, closing the doors simultaneously behind them.

William clambered over his bed, fumbling for his lamp. Its immediate illumination revealed a world of his own making, a wondrous, frightening, fantastic world. Peering from amongst dangling ivy across a wooden beam set high in the dim of the bedroom's ceiling, was a group of inquisitive gargoyles whose figures cast awesome shadows. Hanging from the beam beneath, hairy bats and tiny spiders twirled casually within the room's atmosphere, their beady eyes seeming to peer at the rest of the room's wonders, for poised in corners, parading across bookshelves or standing proudly on the wardrobe, lurked prehistoric monsters, fantastical beasts and characters from world myths. On the uppermost bookshelf a family of mammoths marched in line, while below, peering from behind books, was a pair of reluctant looking dodos, now of course extinct, joining the other creatures in a long lost world. There they all lived again, in the models created by William's own hands, for William was a happy slave to cardboard, glue and paint. In fact any materials that he could lay his hands upon for the purpose of recreation. His current masterpiece was the multi-limbed Indian God, Shiva, lord of the dance. The figure stood gracefully in the belly of a disused fireplace, the mantelpiece of which displayed Hermes, the messenger of the Greek Gods, who gazed out over the youngster's bed.

William threw back the duvet and slipped in, taking a final peep at Hermes before extinguishing the light. His eyes watched the night shadows, his ears listened for any strange sounds, especially breathing. All that was audible was the gentle hoot of an owl from beyond the open window. Slowly his eyelids grew heavy as he sank into the first layer of sleep.

For a while his mind continued to muse over the *something* outside, but he cast it off with reassuring images of the day's events, his walk through the woods and his visit to Mrs Gardner to see how the new goldfish were doing. He was pleased to reflect that Edward, her cat, hadn't touched one. With this thought in mind he slipped deeper into another layer of sleep, then deeper again until he reached a place of absolute rest.

The hands on the bedside clock passed on, eventually reaching the small early hours. William's mind drifted up and down, catching little snippets of dreams passing through.

Then something strange, something mysterious came over him. He felt a slight chill creep over his chest, as if the warmth of his own breath was leaving him. Fearful, he tried to wake, but then he felt his mind and body reel over and drop - drop down and down as if into a bottomless cavern. Again he tried to move but his body had become petrified. Down and down he continued to travel until, eventually, he felt himself bounce, as if in some cradle of suspension.

His curious mind's eye then rolled unnervingly and opened out. At first he could not distinguish anything, for all about him seemed murky and dark. Gradually the blur began to dissipate and he could begin to determine what looked like a filthy hovel. Earthy pots and torn sacks became visible, lit by a small spirited fire that crackled beneath a dented bubbling pot. He could see loose wood shavings upon the ground. Buried amongst them was a pair of dirty feet. William's eye rolled up to peer at the owner of the wretched things and was amazed to see an odd-looking hunchback man with sparse tufts of hair. He had only one heavily lidded pale blue eye and it was fixed on a carving, which, with the aid of crude tools, he was finely chiselling. His beaten face gave a gormless smile as he held the carving up in the dusty light thrown from a small window. The tiny wolf that he held within his chapped hand was indeed perfect.

William observed as the hunchback rose from his seat and shuffled to the rear of the hovel, where bulging, mud, crevice stonewalls held crude shelves supported by thick stakes. Resting upon these were many other carved animals, from tiny rodents to a spectacular antlered deer. The hunchback peered up to the highest shelf, where stood a line of wolves. Straining to reach, he gently placed the smallest of the wolf carvings at the end. It was the baby of the pack. The hunchback stumbled back to admire his completed set of six wolf carvings, led by a magnificent male, a female, and now four of her young.

Suddenly, from the window a large black bird appeared. William recognised it immediately as a raven. The hunchback peered up, smiling at his visitor. William noticed that the hunchback's other eye was firmly sealed by an appalling scar. The raven flapped its way to the hunchback's shoulder. Hugging the bird to his cheek, he sighed as he tickled it beneath its beak.

The hunchback bowed to his shrine of animals before hobbling towards the door of his home. Finding the heavy, rusty old key that dangled from around his neck, he unlocked the door and hauled it open.

Blinding bright rays of light from the world outside immediately fell upon him. His eye winced as he lifted his hand to shun the glare. Clouds loomed across the horizon, for the day was wild and restless. The moors and woodland before him glistened with the damp of fresh rain. He peered out with a childlike attentiveness, for this was a man, at one with nature. He observed his world with an air of hopefulness then smiled, for amidst a clearing, against the darkened sky, could be seen the silhouette of six wolves passing from wood to wood.

The hunchback cupped his hands, bowing respectfully in recognition of their life, their struggle. He had witnessed generations of wolves come and go in that wood. Today, however, as he watched them play, a strange foreboding suddenly gripped him. He touched the scar over the clasped eye - something was about to happen, something thoughtless, something cruel.

The hunchback chided his thoughts and hobbled to the simmering pot. Tonight he would have to eat well, for tomorrow would be an early start on foot to the market. There he would bargain his beautiful carvings for bread and vegetables. All would be going except the wolves. He spooned the hot broth within the pot and ladled a small amount into a bowl while glancing lovingly at the carved wolves. Suddenly an ominous gust of wind heaved its way into the hovel, nearly snatching the door from its hinges and slamming it firmly shut.

William felt alarmed, he tried to pull away from the dream but he couldn't. He saw the hunchback's soulful eye consciously on him, staring within the blackening void. For a few moments William froze, helpless. He then again felt his mind and body drop, drop and surrender itself into another slumber, a shift of sleep that would last until morning.

The curtains of William's room were thrown open.

'Gracious, still in bed!' There was no mistaking Granny's urgent tone. 'I would have thought a boy your age would be out making themselves useful on a Saturday morning. Good-grief!'

'Please Granny, five more minutes,' begged William, as he slipped further under the covers.

'Heavens no,' she chortled, her chin and soft permanently waved hair wobbling comically. With a defiant heave of his duvet she flung it free from the bed.

'Granny!' William pleaded, but she had no time for sleepy heads, her attention had now turned to the Indian God in the fireplace.

'Crikey! What a dust trap we have here.' Her hand reached for the duster beneath her belt. Williams's body jolted in defence.

'No. Please don't touch a thing,' he demanded. 'Remember the octopus?'

'The octopus,' replied Granny reluctantly.

'Yes, *the octopus*,' confirmed William. 'It had eight tentacles and now it only has seven.'

'Seven. I am surprised you can count at all with the sleeping you do,' snorted Granny, without the slightest hint of guilt.

'Ah, yes,' probed William. 'I took particular notice of how clean the remaining seven were - it was you. You're the octopus killer,' he declared, pointing an accusing finger. 'Octopus killer Granny.'

'You shouldn't point, it's rude,' she quibbled, and ambled from the room flicking the duster here and there, only to turn sharply at the door and blow a tight farting noise from her lips before scurrying across the landing.

At breakfast the pungent smell of fish filled the kitchen. His father, Bill Phillips, a well-built, world-weary man with smiling eyes, was eating fresh kippers from Sturminster Market, his floppy fringe dangling like string over his forehead. William looked at the fish gawping up from his father's plate.

'I think I shall have cereal today,' he announced.

'You can't,' shouted Leigh, his younger sister, who looked like a pea from the same pod. 'It's all gone.' She continued to munch even louder on her nibblets of dried corn.

'Well, I'll have toast then,' he retorted, before throwing himself into his chair. Everyone momentarily guffawed, disgusted at William's lacklustre behaviour, before resuming their morning meal.

Jackie Phillips munched on a piece of toast while reading the local newspaper. She peered up at William before dropping her eyes again to finish her read.

'Bread's in the bread bin, toaster's by the wall,' she sang. 'We don't stand on service around here you know.'

Leigh narrowed her eyes at her brother while chomping loudly on the corn.

'Do you think it's because he's hitting puberty?' she said. 'That's why he looks so pale.'

William smirked at his sister and his mother raised the paper.

'William the Pubescent,' quipped Leigh. 'Sounds like a character from history. You should write a story William, featuring yourself as, The Prince Pubescent.'

William stared at his sister's beaming face.

'How about a story called, Princess Leigh, The Not Quite Pubescent?' he snapped.

'That's enough clever talk you two,' said Mrs Phillips as she cracked the paper straight. 'If I'd known my young were going to be comedians, I would have married a circus trainer.'

Amused, William, looked up to catch his mother's last words, only to be horrified at the headlines on the paper's front page.

AXE TO FALL ON GREAT CHERITON WOOD
Council to meet Monday week to discuss and sign final proposals

In disbelief, William read the headline again and again. He was well aware of the possibility of losing his much loved wood, but had always consoled himself with the thought that it couldn't possibly happen, could it? People didn't do things like that in this day and age, did they? He felt sick to his stomach. As the paper started to lean over, William tried to read the article, lowering his head until his chin touched the table.

'I don't believe it!' he blurted. 'I just don't believe it!'

His mother peered from behind the paper's side, pinching her lip guiltily.

'I'm sorry William I knew you'd be upset. I should have mentioned it to you.'

'Tell me what it says?' pleaded William.

Leigh rolled her eyes to her mother and watched her straighten the paper across the table before commencing.

The local town council will be meeting a week on Monday to confirm and sign the final proposals that will seal the fate of Cheriton's ancient Wood.

Bill Phillips looked up from his plate disgruntled. His wife continued:

Mr Marcus Price, who is backing the plan, feels the removal of the wood, in favour of a proposed sight for luxury homes and an up-market shopping and leisure complex will bring much needed wealth into the declining area.

'Some of us are just about making ends meet, we are certainly not "declining". "Declining," how dramatic,' said Mr Phillips, as he dropped another kipper onto his plate. 'I wonder whose coat lining you'll find the money in for *slaughtering* all those trees…his no doubt.'

'He doesn't really own the whole wood, does he?' urged William.

'I'm afraid so,' sighed his mother. 'He has now purchased every acre of it from old Huntley Roach.'

'That Huntly Roach is a bloodsucker. I'm sure some illicit wheeling and dealing went on there,' added Mr Phillips, as he forked a piece of fish into some tomato sauce.

'Evidently Marcus Price is very popular in the village,' said Leigh, 'especially with the ladies.'

Tall, dark and handsome, Marcus Price had indeed charmed the community since moving into the lovely Victorian Courthouse. William had once met him and his son, Sterling, at one of the woodland meetings. For some strange reason, both Sterling and his mother, Chrystal Price, kept themselves to themselves, not really wanting to get to know anyone, which of course only stirred further mystery regarding the 'House of Price.'

Outside in the garden William couldn't help but fall into a state of despair. The bright warm sun on his face, the sound of the bees busily making honey, and the sweet smell of honeysuckle that fragranced the air, for once meant nothing to his senses - they were drowned in a wave of misery. He sat on some stone steps, his imagination now fired up with the ugly images of bulldozers ripping and tearing away at the fragile life of the wood. He felt helpless. Nellie the collie dog peered at him from the entrance of her kennel, not the friendliest of pets, unless a biscuit or football presented itself within easy reach. He watched her pluck an old bone from the obscurity of her den and gnaw on it furiously. William knew that every type of domestic dog, both large and small, is a descendant of the wolf. His mind then flashed - the wolves…the hunchback…the dream. Yes, the dream. It felt so strange, somehow so real. What on earth did it all mean? Was it some kind of message? If so, for whom? William felt a sudden overwhelming urge to visit Great Cheriton Wood - perhaps there he would find a clue.

His thoughts were broken by the sound of a dramatic, screaming sneeze from somewhere inside the house. Had his Granny sneaked in yet again to clean? The Indian God, Shiva, with his many arms, would be like a skittle alley for Granny and duster to roll down. Worried, he peered up towards his bedroom window, only to see with relief the living room window open, as his granny poked out a duster and shook it violently.

'I hope they pay you well here Mrs Phillips,' came a jovial voice from beyond the garden gate. Blue-eyed, sandy-haired Tommy Andrews was leaning on the frame making a lazy rocking motion, the sun warming his face. He was the farm hand who normally worked during the week. Bill Phillips, however, had plans this morning to prepare the wagons in readiness for the summer haymaking.

Granny Phillips huffed farcically.

'Struth, you'd be lucky to get a penny voucher from this lot. I always said Bill should have gone into banking... Mind you, I don't suppose it helped him failing his math level one.'

Tommy Andrews pushed open the gate and plodded into the garden.

'I don't suppose you lot have heard the news then!' he announced.

Granny Phillips snivelled.

'As you know full well Tommy, it is within accordance that good characters like myself are above gossip.'

'Very respectful of you Mrs Phillips,' said Tommy, taking lazy steps toward the back door. 'You'll not want to hear what Mrs Bramble has to say then.'

Mrs Bramble was Granny Phillips' archrival at bingo.

'Mrs Bramble you say,' said Granny, stuffing the duster keenly beneath her belt. 'Considering the news bears knowledge of an acquaintance, it would be good and proper to receive it justly so…Tommy, give us the news sharpish please.'

'Well, it appears, according to Mrs Bramble that is, that Judith Tench suddenly went missing last night. Nobody knows where.'

William shivered at Tommy's report.

'Missing?' exclaimed Granny Phillips. 'What do you mean?'

'Well, it's reckoned that late last night, her daughter, Livia, found the house open and empty, and that some table was knocked over that had a brandy glass on it. Spilled it did, all over the carpet, like blood. Police have been called and all.'

'Crikey!' gasped Granny Phillips. 'Now there's a stain she'll have trouble removing when she turns up.'

'If she does,' added William. 'If the police are involved, it must be serious.'

'Goes to show,' concluded Tommy. 'A thriller could actually take place within our very midst!' He winked at Mrs Phillips who shot rapidly back inside as Tommy strode toward the kitchen leaving young William with his mind racing. Something felt uncomfortably wrong. He made to find his bike.

Chapter 2

Revelation

The family of swallows nesting high in the rafters of the cowshed watched inquisitively as William assembled his bicycle from its temporary rest. He walked it to the farm's drive and was about to mount the saddle when he determined the urgent clip of his neighbour's hard shoes. Withdrawing himself behind the cover of some rusty corrugated sheets, he peeped to view Miss Pike, a prickly lady who would vent her frustrations on those first seen. She always wore grey, matching her hair, which was tied in an extremely tight-looking knot. Her thrifty little figure paced beady-eyed to the backdoor. William couldn't help but laugh wickedly to himself when he saw his Granny answer it, broom in hand. She was soon joined by his mother to hear Miss Pike, who had come yet again to complain about Nellie using her garden for a short cut to the children's playing fields. Having been satisfied with a chorus of, 'so sorry,' 'well of course' and 'naughty Nellie,' she went on her way. William then seized the opportunity to make towards the woods, chased down the farm drive by the rebel herself, Nellie, who for some bizarre reason had a dangerous fascination for spinning wheels.

Peddling purposefully through Cheriton, past the homes of various villagers, some of whom he knew, William headed for the woods. He had just passed Wisteria Lane when his mind filled with the news of Judith Tench. He pressed his brakes lightly and the bike gave a whistle-like piping sound as it ground to a halt. Steadying himself upon the road, William, within the peace of the village thumbed the handlebars rubber grips whilst considering the houses before him. Judith Tench's house was set a little distance back from the others but was fairly easy to view from the raised ground upon which it was built. William sidestepped his bike and allowed himself to drift down the hill until Judith's house was visible.

The front lawn was level with his chin, making it easy for him to hug himself against the wall beneath. He peered through the jagged stones that were imbedded like teeth along its front. Through some open French windows he could see the striking slim figure of Judith's daughter, Livia, moving an ornate chair. Livia Tench sometimes resided at her mother's house when she was between boyfriends, so to speak. Rumour had it that she had a fair number of admirers. A mobile phone started to trill loudly. Livia plucked it from the pocket of her tight jeans whilst throwing back her dark red locks.

'Yes...oh, hello darling...Well, the police have just left...No, I didn't ...What? You want me to look for it now....O.K, I'll do the best I can...Love you too.'

She snapped the phone shut and sat thoughtfully upon the chair, stroking the side of her temples anxiously. Suddenly, she caught sight of William's face behind the toothy stones. She stared hard into his inquisitive eyes before rising from her seat to close the French windows firm. Embarrassed, William threw himself upon his bike and made for his intended destination, Great Cheriton Wood.

Beyond the sea-like stretch of a lush field rose the ancient wood, its outer trees appearing like plumped-up pillows, while beneath their shade the inner depths beckoned.

Having rested his bike, William gently pulled up the barbed wire fence surrounding the wood and swung underneath. At last he was within his hallowed ground. He walked between the trees, which shrouded him in speckled light. A light breeze made the leaves rustle refreshingly, a sensation that lifted his spirits above the earlier bleak news. Within the woodland canopies, squirrels leapt from branch to branch and he could see tiny tree-creeping birds working their way around thick mossy bark. In the distance he could hear the sound of a woodpecker hammering ardently away, its gentle pummelling trailing into a pleasant echo. Here in the woods William felt totally happy. His imagination could take him anywhere, he could be anyone - a prehistoric man away from the safety of his cave, wary of the sabre-toothed tiger or a Greek hero of legend on a mission to slay a Gorgon.

Breathing in the smell of fresh sap that hung in the air, for a while his mind was free from worry and he paced happily towards the woodland's heart, heading for the most sacred of his hangouts.

At the centre of a peaceful, hazy clearing, in which dandelion seeds floated aimlessly, stood his favourite tree, a spectacular, lonely dead oak, its slanting posture making it easy to climb. Here William could sit alone amongst the ivy and wonder about the way of the world...and the wolves. He had read much about wolves, in reference books and myths, where there they were portrayed as guardians. He knew that the native North Americans always regarded them as teachers not enemies, and that they never killed humans. However, since Europeans had settled in North America, William was aware they had killed over two million wolves.

It was then that a dainty spider, busily weaving a web, caught his attention. He watched for a while, fascinated by its determined labour, but it wasn't long before clouds of doom descended upon him, for the truth was, in a matter of days the wood and its life would be no more.

His eyes dropped unconsciously to his watch as if time was saying 'hello.' The hands had moved faster than he would have allowed and he realised that he needed to be going soon. Foraging his way down the old oak, he followed the track back to his bicycle and started for home.

Travelling through the village he caught sight of his elderly friend Mrs Gardner watering the plants outside her cottage.

'Hello, Mrs Gardner,' he smiled.

She spun round, raised her right hand to her brow and saluted him gallantly.

'Good day William, and how are you this fine afternoon?'

'Oh, I'm all right,' he mumbled.

'Oh, no you're not,' she replied knowingly. 'You have a face as long as a whale. Come in for tea and we shall have a chat. Edward is in, he'll cheer you up.'

Edward the cat, in all his ginger splendour, sat proudly in the small elegant living room. Mrs Gardner's well set but neat figure perched trimly on a stool. Aways looking smart, her blonde hair was in a bun and her small pearl necklace dangled daintily as she poured tea.

'So what beat is the drum playing this time William? Have we risen above or dropped below three? Is the Gulf Steam about to cease motion? Will the planet self-combust, or form an ice pack and preserve us all?'

'It's the wood Mrs Gardner. It really does look like we're going to lose it after all.'

Mrs Gardner appeared reflective for a moment.

'I'm sorry William, not just for you but for everything. Billions of trees worldwide, every year, are being destroyed for profit. People have forgotten, or are ignorant, about how life on Earth works! Cheriton's trees, along with all the others, make up the planet's vital organs. They help us breathe.' She placed the teapot on the tray. 'However, all is not lost…there's still time to raise a conscience.' The china teacups clinked sweetly as Mrs Gardner handed William his drink. 'Do you ever have feelings William?'

William felt a little taken aback by the question.

'How do you mean? Like what?'

'Well, sometimes people have a feeling, a sense that something's about to happen. We call it insight…a knowing.'

'Well, yes…recently Granny and I were playing cards and I had a feeling that I knew her hand exactly, which wasn't particularly good as she still won.'

Mrs Gardener laughed.

'Knowing is one thing, skill is another.' She looked thoughtfully into her delicate cup. 'I feel something incredible is about to happen William, and you are going to have to be prepared.'

'What?' he asked. But Mrs Gardner just drank her tea and smiled.

William glanced out of the window. He could barely see the world outside for the Virginia creeper growing over the glass. Looking around the living room, his eyes rested on a dragon perched on top of a grandfather clock that stood behind Mrs Gardner. Its long neck and tail were arched upwards to meet each other forming a perfect circle.

'I see you're looking at the dragon,' observed Mrs Gardner. 'It's very old. It represents the circle of life. What goes around, comes around. What you send out, so you get back...all is eternal.' She reached for the teapot. 'Now William, another cup of tea?'

The road home past the church was steep, so William walked beside his bike and mulled over Mrs Gardner's words. What could he possibly have to prepare for, the loss of the wood perhaps? Shade from the roadside trees darkened his sunny face and he felt a chill run through his body as if ice had stroked his veins. He was approaching the church and could see the old eighteenth century stocks poised outside its gates. William wondered if criminals had ever truly been shackled to them. He smiled as an image of himself, locked at the ankle, coloured his imagination. His granny was standing before him clutching a cabbage and several eggs.

'Oh, William, to hear that you planned to lay siege to the town council, and all for a few blessed trees, really.' She looked at the produce in her hands. 'Do you think they'll be delivering any more groceries here?' she sniffed cheekily, before trotting home.

William dropped his face to the ground grinning, only to be shaken from his warm dream by the thump of the church door. He peered up to see his neighbour, Miss Pike, step nervously from its porch, dip a gloved hand into her handbag and draw out what looked like a hanky. She dabbed its folds across each cheek, snivelled heavily and looked to the sky.

'Oh, God forgive me...for what I'm about to do...please forgive me!' she begged before stepping down the church path.

William suddenly felt the urge to hide. His panicked eyes shot from tree to tree. Beside the church stood the manor gates. He hauled the bike and himself promptly behind them.

Squatting behind a dilapidated wall, he rose to glimpse Miss Pike, who was now passing through the graveyard's gates, peering uneasily about herself as if fearful of being seen. Satisfied that all was safe, she pulled the hem of her jacket straight and trotted stiffly towards home. William had never seen Miss Pike as worried as that, and although he wasn't sure, he didn't believe her to be a regular attendee of the church. And as for tears, he felt they were something she couldn't possibly draw. But most baffling of all, was why she should be asking for forgiveness. The woman was obviously frightened, but frightened of what? He watched her fragile figure disappear up through the lane before reaching for his bike. Angling it out of the manor's drive, he threw his leg over the saddle and began to work his way home. What he didn't know was that out from a cluster of trees behind, their shade dim and concealing, slid the figure of a young man dressed in tattered denim. The observer was being observed.

Again that night the moon shone brightly. William felt restless within his room. He busied himself with some dental work on the jaw of a Tyrannosaurus Rex while peering reluctantly at his clock. He felt tired, but last nights experience had tainted his want of sleep with fear. His bed was now a prison, in which he would soon have to retire. There was no way he was going to put that landing light on, no way. He did, however, drop shamefully to his knees to check under the bed, scolding himself afterwards. This was not the behaviour of a thirteen-year-old.

At last he climbed into bed, pulling his duvet about him. At least checking under the bed had given him some feeling of peace, and it wasn't long before he fell into a deep, irrepressible slumber.

The clock by his bed passed 11 o'clock, 12 o'clock, and one. William stirred cosily, satisfied that all was well before travelling off into another sleepy patch. Then, somewhere around two,

William's mind began to wander. At first he felt in control of the sensations and was happy to flirt with the experience - that was until he felt his whole being topple horrendously backward as if he was turning up side down. His stomach seemed to lurch into his mouth, his body shot cold, as down and down he dropped, down into the bottomless chasm as before. Although petrified, this time William felt he could sense more, as vast spectrums of light seemed to speed past him, their rays seeming to darken the further he fell, until boom - again he bounced within the strange womb of suspension where for a moment he thought he could hear an echo of distant cries.

Once again, unnervingly, his mind's eye opened up to explore. At first, all that was visible was a hazy mist, but as its vapours began to clear, William could once again distinguish the figure of the hunchback man hobbling across the moors. He was clutching a small sack. The light was beginning to fade, giving way to the arrival of a dark storm. William could distinguish a disciplined procession of about twenty men on horseback, followed by a horse-drawn cart bearing a large empty cage. The hunchback seemed to observe these visitors with caution. Suddenly, as if a great fear rose in his heart, he raced back to his home, only to find that the door had been broken and torn down. Desperately he searched inside, but nothing had been touched. His stool and tools were just as he had left them. Then he looked towards the shelves, running his eye along them, stopping in shock - the wolves had gone.

Suddenly, loud squawks came from outside. The hunchback staggered out to see his faithful raven in flight, squawking loud bellows of alarm, for coming over the round of a hill could be seen an army of men on horseback galloping towards them down into the shallow of a hill. At first it looked as if dogs were at the forefront of a possible hunt, but as the scene grew nearer, the dreadful truth began to unfold - the men were indeed hunters and they were hunting the wolves.

The storm was beginning to grow angry. Heavy clouds, black and blue, began to thicken, releasing darts of hard rain upon the landscape. The wolves had now been driven further down the hill towards a swollen river. The entourage of men on horseback now began to spread out, encircling the family. There was no escape, only the great rapids of the river before them. The ground lit up with the forks of lightening that sprang across the sky. A single horseman, the leader, drew forward, his flaring black eyes glaring eagerly at the helpless creatures before him.

'Hold them. Cut them off!' he bawled.

The thunder cracked a deep resounding blow. The wolves, now at the mouth of the intense flood, had no choice but to relinquish themselves to the baying screams of the gathering men. Terrified, the wolves huddled together. Across the river, the hunchback, desperate, had hobbled to the scene, his rags drenched with rain. He stared knowingly at the glaring leader.

'Leave them!' he stammered. 'Let them be! You know not what you do...I *beg* you!'

The leader's face darkened. He drew his sword and laughed, his mirth drowned by the deep rumble of the immense storm. The horsemen closed in, tightening their grasp.

The master wolf turned to face his family - he would not let their fate be left to Man. With a courageous leap, he plunged into the rage of the river. The others watched trembling. Then the she-wolf approached the water's edge, beckoning her pups to follow. The men screamed wildly as they watched her throw herself in. The pups, now alone, huddled together petrified, their tiny ears pinched fearful against their heads. Mustering strength the eldest peered at his struggling mother before drawing the faith to follow. The frenzied men leapt from their horses and drew nearer, their arms outstretched. But the remaining young would not allow themselves to be grasped. Each in turn jumped into the angry rapids as the men plummeted to the ground, their hands empty.

The water engulfed their bodies. All but their heads managed to break the surface, as they pushed and pulled against the river's powerful flow. But the relentless current was far too strong and in a desperate effort to find their strength and reach the other side, the frightened and exhausted pups, one by one, succumbed to the river's depths. Their mother and father soldiered on, but the loss of their young and their draining vigour weighed far too heavily on their hearts and with a final cry of despair, they gave in to the river's forceful flow. The thunder roared as the waters drew them down, snatching their lives without regard.

'No!' sobbed the broken-hearted hunchback, stumbling over the sodden ground. 'You know not what you do!'

The restless horses on the other side trod hard and heavy at the riverbank, their tempers strained by the callous jeering men on their backs.

'No!' again wailed the hunchback. 'This shall not be!'

With those words and as much emotion as the storm itself, he tore the glistening key from around his neck, screaming wildly as he cast it high above the violent waters.

'Mark this act,' he cried. 'Mark this act on those I love!'

The men on the other side watched in awe as the key rose. A bolt of lightening struck it directly, causing sparks so bright and intense they pierced the sky. Arrows of light swiftly dispersed, leaving the key to fall and drop deep beneath the raging torrent below.

William's startled eyes opened wide. With the revelation of what he had just seen, his body trembled. He had been given an insight. He felt that something lay deep within the woods, a mystery that would only now start to fully enfold. The legacy of the six wolves had begun.

Chapter 3

The Quest

Stirred by the sound of sharp spits against his bedroom window, William pulled himself from the cocoon of his cosy bed to investigate the disturbance. Peering through the slit in his curtains he could see Nellie's tail wagging excitedly while his mischievous sister foraged amongst the shrubbery for more tiny stones. Standing beside her, hands on hips, was her classmate and best friend, Alphonza Pink.

Twelve year old Alphonza had been living on the west side of the village for a few years now, having moved down from the city after the break up of her mother Rosie's marriage. A very laid-back but clued up young girl, she and her mother found the peace that Cheriton offered suited both their temperaments. Her short-cut, black afro-hair glistened in the morning sun and she smiled when the corner of her eye caught the rustle of William's curtains.

'Well, and a good morning to ya young Master William Phillips,' she cooed in a mock Southern American drawl. 'Is you getting a lazy boy there Master William? Now Alphonza here can't go a marrying no lazy boy, I yon guess she'll have to look elsewhere for more appropriate suitors.'

Behind the thickness of her glasses William could see her teasing eyes hiding a smile.

'Don't be too mean Alphonza,' quipped Leigh. 'He has come to greet you from yonder bedroom window wearing only his underpants.'

The two girls huddled together like giggling mice, while William, embarrassed, groped for the ends of the curtains.

Their mirth was soon interrupted by snappy barks from Nellie who darted to the garden gate to find Alphonza's mother, Rosie Pink, wrestling nervously with the latch. She was a hearty, plump lady with an infectious laugh. The smile she usually wore, however, was replaced with an expression of grave concern. Nellie had a soft spot for Rosie and leapt playfully upon her outrageous bright white and red polka-dot summer dress.

'Down Nellie, down!' she begged. 'Your paw marks won't match my dots honey.' Rosie, now laughing uncontrollably, searched inside her handbag for a sweet to satisfy the little dog, finally presenting a purple- wrapped chocolate jewel before Nellie's nose.

'Get down you riotous mutt!' came a gruff voice. Rosie looked up, much relieved to see Bill Phillips striding towards her.

'Oh, hello Bill. I'm sorry to disturb you but I need to tell someone to put my mind at rest.'

'Whatever's the matter?' asked the girls intrigued.

'It's Miss Pike. She's gone! I can't find her anywhere. When I arrived about an hour ago I just found the house open with nobody in. I only clean her house once a month and you know Miss Pike, I have to be there dead on the hour, only then will she unbolt the door for me.' Rosie was the only person in the whole area who would actually clean for the woman.

'Another missing person,' said an excited Leigh. 'Just like Judith Tench last week. Something's going down!'

'Let's not jump to any conclusions,' said Mr Phillips scratching back his salt and pepper hair. 'Let Rosie and I go down to Miss Pike's and investigate further. Everyone else had better stay here. If she turns up and finds her house filled with intruders, she'll have us thrown against a wall and shot...so to speak.'

Rosie gasped at the thought and followed Bill obediently.

Jackie Phillips had her hands in the kitchen sink, busily peeling potatoes while the youngsters sat around the table sipping cold lemonade. Now fully dressed, William had joined them. His head was full of the dream he'd had the night before and he had a strange feeling the ladies going missing and the dream were connected, yet his mind boggled to think how.

'They have been gone an hour now,' said Mrs Phillips, amid the sound of swift scrapes from her potato peeler. 'They can't be sipping sherry, not at Miss Pike's. Something's definitely wrong.'

'Perhaps she's gone fishing,' joked Leigh.

'More like looked in the mirror for the first time in years,' said Alphonza. 'Horrified, she's shot off on her broomstick for a quick facial.'

As they giggled shamefully around the table, two shadows appeared at the door. Bill and Rosie had returned to report that things were a little more serious than anticipated. Not only had the house been entered, but some objects had been discovered in the pantry that were so disturbing, Rosie didn't wish to discuss anything further.

The police were telephoned whilst strong tea was served to console everyone's bewildered and startled nerves. More potatoes were peeled for the Pink's, who had accepted an invitation to stay for lunch. Granny Phillips had appeared and promptly occupied herself sweeping the garden path.

The morning passed on and in a short time Constable Stone arrived to investigate and clarify certain details. He was a tall man with a bulbous, ruddy face, a high-pitched singsong voice, and an amusing swaying body movement. Having gathered as much information as he could, as well as tea, he finally left, only to return seconds later to ask if he could possibly spend a penny.

A little later than usual, lunch was finally served. William happily carved the chicken whilst his father deliberated over which of his homemade wines to serve. Eventually plumping for the rhubarb, he filled Rosie's and his mother's glasses before pouring his own. Rosie had calmed down and was now enjoying herself immensely. Granny Phillips' dry sense of humour, which got drier the more she drank, amused her no end. The roast was devoured by one and all with as much clamour and joyous laughter as the Knights at the Round Table. The two chatty ladies exchanged tales of cleaning conquests.

'Now if you think it takes courage to clean Miss Pike's house,' declared Rosie, 'tomorrow's cleaning assignment fills me with even greater dread!'

'Why?' enquired Granny Phillips.   Who do you work for tomorrow?'

'Marcus Price!' exclaimed Rosie.

William suddenly caught the conversation and listened keenly as Rosie continued.

'I guess I shouldn't be talking about the people I work for like this but sometimes he really unnerves me. Normally he's a very charming man, but then you see a sudden change of character, and it's as if he's someone else. It was only last week I made the terrible mistake of going into the 'get out room.'

'The "get out room?"' asked William, curious.

'Oh yes,' said Rosie, as she took another sip of rhubarb wine for courage. 'It's at the very top of the stairs. I call it the 'get out room,' because that's what he bellowed at me, "Get out, get out!" I had literally only touched the handle. I was petrified. Whatever's in that room, he sure don't want people to know.'

After coffee was served Rosie decided to not stay too long into the afternoon, as there was her own housework to do. William, wanting to share the experience of the drowning wolves with Mrs Gardner, offered to escort Rosie, with a view to visiting Ivy Cottage upon his return. After changing her elegant footwear to athletic pumps, Rosie was happily off. William felt that this was an ideal opportunity to enquire more about the House of Price, of which he felt his curiosity growing, particularly with regard to Marcus.

'Rosie, I know it's not my business to ask, but tell me more about Mr Price, what you know of him, where he's from, and what's his past?

Rosie's eyes rolled warily to William.

'You know, charm aside, there is something strange about the man. I always feel troubled working there. Sometimes the atmosphere feels very oppressive. It's sad because his wife,

Chrystal, is such a lovely girl. But I sense something dark in that house.'

William self-consciously kicked a stray stone that petered off into a crack in the road.

'Apart from the "get out room," is there anything else you feel oddly about? His son Sterling, for instance, what's he like?'

'I know only what I feel, William. The family are very reserved, although I did see Sterling in tears one morning. He was babbling about some change of name.'

'Change of name,' probed William. 'From what?'

Rosie shrugged. 'I don't know, but I can tell you he's not an altogether happy boy.'

William looked down at the sun-drenched grey road thinking about the information Rosie had given him. He could sense the late afternoon becoming duskier earlier than was usual. His father always said the days grew shorter immediately the youngsters broke up from school.

Having said his goodbyes to Rosie, he changed his direction and headed towards Ivy Cottage. In the distance William could hear Bob Gloster's ice-cream van piping a dulcet tune. All the while his mind was filled with a sense of the unknown and he could hear in his head the words of Mrs Gardner: "Something is about to happen, William." For a moment he felt nervously giddy.

Outside the cottage Edward was sprawled out, bathing in the soft sun.

'Hello Edward, you beach bum.'

Edward looked up indignantly, lazily drew to his feet and sauntered off through the side-gate that led into the back garden. William followed him, happy to find Mrs Gardner standing by the garden pond studiously pruning some rosebushes.

'Good evening, dear William. Any news about Miss Pike?'

'Nothing,' said William. 'How did you know?'

'Members of the tribe dear boy, the selfless, they're everywhere. Word gets round.' she smiled.

'You know what Mrs Gardner, I feel that these people going missing are connected.'

Mrs Gardner looked totally absorbed in her task of purposefully deadheading the rose bush. William suddenly felt a little distance in his heart.

'Cut off the old heads you see, to make way for the new. There's many a new bud in this bush,' mumbled Mrs Gardner to herself.

William took a breath and pushed further with his thoughts.

'There's something I want to share with you. Last night and the night before, I had a strange dream. But I'm not actually sure it was a dream.'

Mrs Gardner turned her head towards him and peered above her half-glasses looking as if she were suddenly coming to her senses.

'Attention Gardner!' she snapped, 'Master William has news and here you are fiddling with rose bushes.' She rested a hand upon the head of a dilapidated statue of which William was fond, for it represented the Greek Goddess of wisdom, Athena, complete with an owl perched on its shoulder. 'Right William, let's have a full report.'

For the first time William was ready to unburden himself of the heavy dream, but before he could continue there came a sudden loud crash of glass from inside Ivy Cottage. They both looked up in alarm.

'Quick William...behind me and in line...something's afoot. Let's investigate.'

With stealth they both crept to the cottage and entered the back door. Except for the light drip of a tap, they were enveloped by silence. Ears as sharp as fox's, they made their way carefully through to the hall. There came another crash followed by a heavy bump.

'Someone's upstairs William,' whispered Mrs Gardner. 'In line and hold fast. Oh, and hand me one of those brollies from the rack.'

William dutifully complied and they both started to ascend the staircase as quietly as possible, Mrs Gardner armed with a brolly. Another bump and crash reverberated from above.

'Something's in the loft,' declared Mrs Gardner. 'Quick William, the steps.'

They both gathered the steps from the spare room and assembled them. Mrs Gardner climbed them briskly and reached for the latch of the loft door.

'Be careful please, Mrs Gardner!' implored William.

As another smash of glass came from above, Mrs Gardner threw the loft door open and peered through. Apart from a galaxy of dust swimming in the light thrown from an open roof window, there was no sign of an intruder. Perhaps they're hiding, she thought, as she launched herself up through the loft entrance, William following. The space was full of old tea chests, two of which had fallen over. Fragments of shattered glass had spilled onto the floor.

'There's definitely been a disturbance,' said William pulling himself up into the small space. Mrs Gardner's eyes inspected nooks and crannies. Finding no sign of life, she started to replace the contents thrown from the chests.

'Funny thing that window being open William, I don't remember leaving it so,' she reflected. 'Perhaps one of Edward's neighbours called, you know some cats have very strange social habits.'

William helped to retrieve items that had fallen some distance from the chests, handing them to Mrs Gardner. He then paused, for the final object he held suddenly caught his eye. Within a blanket of newspaper he could distinguish a small animal, its tiny nose protruding from the end of the roll. Mrs Gardner noticed William's curiosity with the package.

'Open it up if you like, let's see what's inside.' William untied the string carefully.

'All the items in these chests belonged to my late husband, Arthur. He was an historian and traveller. Anything old he loved.' Her eyes grew dreamy. 'He believed that every object held a story. Just hold something in your hands and you will sense its past.'

The string dropped to the floor and William un-wrapped the object. His eyes grew wide, his whole body shivered, the hairs on the back of his neck stood up, for there, resting in the palm of his hand, was a small carved wolf.

'I don't believe it. It's one of the pups from my dream. But how, why?'

Mrs Gardner looked up.

'This being the dream you had last night and the night before?'

'Yes, you see…' Before he could continue, back in the darkness of the corner came another loud smash. Startled, they both turned round but could see nothing. Mrs Gardner was about to whisper but was stopped in her tracks by the strange sound of clawing feet on the floor. Something was hiding at the rear of the attic, but what? Mrs Gardner stood up, so defiantly she banged her head on the beam above.

'Come out!' she ordered. 'Whoever you are, show yourself!'

There followed a moment's silence, then suddenly, a large black form appeared as if from nowhere, launching itself upon the biggest Indian tea chest. William and Mrs Gardner fell back in awe as they stared transfixed at the magnificent shimmering raven before them. Its intense round eye peered at them from the side of its head. All three of them exchanged looks of marvel. The large bird then stretched out, threw back its head and squawked six times before finally opening its wings and with one single flap jumping to the window. Turning for one final glance at William, the bird dropped from the window into flight. William leapt after it, his hands grabbing the window's edge to haul himself up. Mrs Gardner quickly cupped her hands beneath his knee for added support.

'What can you see William?'

William looked out across the facing fields. In the distance he could see the now tiny figure of the raven disappearing over the vicinity of Great Cheriton Wood.

'It's all right Mrs Gardner, you can loose your hold now, I'm coming back in.' His trainers plumped to the floor. 'The wolf…the raven…the dream…Oh Mrs Gardner, I've lots to tell you.'

'Well come on!' she replied. 'Let's get that kettle on. Bring the pup with you and we'll talk.'

Mrs Gardner chinked her cup onto its saucer, placing it on the tray for a refill.

'So you say that after the wolves were drowned the hunchback took the key from about his neck and threw it into the river?'

'Yes…and then the dream ended.'

Mrs Gardner looked longingly at the wooden wolf pup now poised on the tea tray.

'I feel that an inheritance has been passed down to you William, and you have been specially chosen to deliver it. You are about to embark on a quest, for what I cannot be sure. That's for you to discover.'

For the first time in his life William felt an overwhelming sense of responsibility. He wasn't quite sure if he wanted it, but then a passage into the unknown is never comfortable.

'The wolf is yours William, I want you to have it.'

'But it's something that once belonged to Mr Gardner, I couldn't!'

'It's only a possession. I remember Arthur finding it at a local antique's fair. We had such a lovely day. Its rediscovery has already brought me a fond memory. You were meant to have it, William. Its time in this house is now over.'

She placed the pup in William's hands. He held it with great appreciation.

'Did you know wolves mate for life, and their pups stay with their family for about two years?'

Mrs Gardner's face warmed with approval.

'Too many advisors can send one to despair. Keep things close to your heart at this time William. Be careful who you share your experiences with. If you have any real worries, just come and see me.'

'Don't worry, I will,' said William.

'Good,' announced Mrs Gardner. 'Right I think it's time for a tea total toast don't you?' They both raised their cups and saucers and Mrs Gardner lifted her chin.

'To the adventure that's about to begin.' 'Chink.'

Placing the pup safely within the rucksack at the rear of his bike, William grabbed the handlebars and shifted into the middle of the road. With much to contemplate he felt a sense of elation, and in order to exercise his thoughts, he chose a longer route home.

Again, at various points the road towards Beech Tree Farm was quite steep and William felt it necessary to walk the bike, staring as he did at the shadows cast by the roadside trees. Looking further ahead he could see the old rectory at the base of a small brow and could hear the sound of voices in amiable chatter. Drawing closer and pausing by the cover of a weeping willow tree, he could distinguish the Reverend Gillespie and his wife, and the man behind the looming removal of the wood, Marcus Price. The Reverend, hands in his pockets, was laughing, his creased eyes appearing like little slits while his wife, a tall lady, who always wore brown tweed even in high-summer, refastened a slide in her unkempt grey hair.

'Lovely to see you again Marcus,' she guffawed. 'We really ought to do the antique stalls together sometime. Who knows what we'll find?'

Marcus Price bowed his handsome head.

'Indeed, let me know when you're free and I shall find the time.' He offered his hand. 'Well, it's good to see you both again and looking so well. Goodbye for now, and see you soon.'

The Gillespie's returned graceful smiles as Marcus Price jumped into his Range Rover. He pulled out of the Rectory's leafy, copper beech drive and was about to pass William on his bike when suddenly the vehicle ground to a halt and the electric window nearest to him drew further down.

'Hope I didn't startle you there,' said Mr Price apologetically. 'Your face looks familiar and although I've seen many, I never forget a face. Do you mind my asking your name?'

Caught off guard, William felt a little nervous but mustered a polite smile.

'Phillips, my name is William Phillips.'

'Ah, yes,' returned Price. 'You and your family live up at the old farm. I remember you now. You were at the woodland meeting some weeks ago. Showed great concern, if I recollect. Well, William, I do share your worries, but that land is laying waste. Think of the opportunities it'll give everyone…work, leisure, homes.'

'I understand Mr Price, but according to some people at the meeting, those homes you'll build will be far beyond the affordability for many of the folks around here. A roof over your head is a necessity not a luxury!'

'William, I am aware of that, but we do need to think of the economy.
It's from that that we all thrive. Money, wealth is very important and if the bottom drops so to speak, we'd all be in terrible trouble!'

'Yes, but not as deep as the trouble we'll all be in if we continue to rob the world of its natural resources…that wood is invaluable!'

Marcus Price closed his long lashed eyes and smiled. 'I can see that you're a very bright young man, William, and I truly admire your acumen. But I don't expect for one moment that you fully understand the necessity for progress.'

'Ok, but as my granddad always said, progress wouldn't be progress unless it's fairly criticised - you can't have one voice moving in one direction!' William blushed. He felt he was gabbling.

Marcus Price gave a polite glance at his watch.

'Well, William, it's nice to talk and I'd really like to put the world to rights with you but I simply must dash. Do give your family my regards. See you again soon, no doubt. Goodbye.'

William watched the vehicle's window rise, veiling Price's face. He could see why members of the village were so charmed, but there was something about this meeting that puzzled him. He felt, strangely, that he had known Price from sometime before. His face held a ring of familiarity, an uncanny familiarity.

William shivered as he observed the Range Rover motor down the road. He felt resolved. He didn't want to live in Mr Price's world, a world that would tear up his wood and further pollute the very natural fabric from which we had all come. Who would really win and who would really lose? He kicked the pedal up on his bicycle, left the cover of the weeping willow and sped home.

Chapter 4

Fear

The wolf pup looked quite at home perched upon William's bedroom mantelpiece. Stepping back to appreciate the display, he cupped his hands beneath his nose wondering where the other five could possibly be.

The house was very quiet that Sunday evening, a pleasant yet unnerving quiet, as if tomorrow were swelling behind fastened doors. Finding his father in the living room wrestling with the Sunday papers, William asked where everyone had gone.

'They're all next door at Miss Pike's,' he replied, as a page of his paper began to tilt. 'She's still not shown up yet. Constable Stone called round again with a colleague. You can go down there if you wish but under no circumstances are you and the girls to enter the back pantry.' Without hesitation William took off.

Arriving at Miss Pike's front lawn, William discovered a triumphant exhibition from Nellie who, with ferocious glee, was shaking a punctured football to and fro, making air gasp from tense slits. Inside the sadly withdrawn house, Mrs Phillips was writing the name, Pike, on a set of keys.

'Oh, there you are,' she mused. 'I was wondering where you had got to. You've just missed Constable Stone. We are to check the house until further news. I don't believe Miss Pike had any known relatives. Constable Stone is entrusting us with the keys.'

William had never seen inside Miss Pike's house before and like the others he was curious.

'Just slipping upstairs to check the bathroom and landing windows,' said his mother leaving him alone.

William crept into the sparsely lit sitting room, his eyes wandering over its sleepy décor. The stripped yellowing papered walls held heavy framed paintings of prudish looking Victorian children dressed in frills, their canvases darkened with age. There was a rather tired looking baby grand piano in one corner with a lace draped over its body. From its thread dangled a tiny spider. William remembered his Granddad Jack mentioning that he used to hear Miss Pike play it happily when he himself was a young man. But now it lay still, lost in time with everything else. Through an open door William could see another door firmly shut. Could that be the pantry, he thought? He remembered his father's words but his curiosity was too strong to withhold. Glancing toward the stairs, he could hear the echo of inquisitive chatter from his sister and Alphonza. He thought for a moment, then, intrigued by the door, he turned. Heart thumping, he paced towards it.

There was minimal light in this area of the house and having only half opened the door, William had trouble deciphering what lay the other side. Pushing it wider, he was suddenly startled by a handful of flies that seemed to spawn from an earthenware sink. Disturbed, they hovered in the stifling air, air that had the vague smell of something putrid lingering within. William winced as he waved the flies from his face before peering into the sink's belly. It was here that his eyes widened with surprise. Poised in a corner of the sink was a white waxen doll moulded into the figure of a man. Beside it lay a knife and goblet, both of which looked as if they had been suddenly dropped. William stared perplexed. Spilling from the goblet was a reddish-looking fluid, dripping into the void of the plughole. Curious, he dipped his finger in to examine it closer. Cold to the touch, the fluid dribbled creepily down his skin as he held his fingers up to inspect it.

William shivered - it was blood.

Unnerved, he drew back from the sink. Had Miss Pike been practising witchcraft? But why, thought William? Whatever had possessed her to do such a thing? He then recollected her leaving the church the previous morning asking for forgiveness. The waxen doll was an image of someone, someone that perhaps she wanted to see dead. Clutching his mouth he backed out of the pantry.

Leaning up against an immediate wall, he stared blankly at the sunlit piano. But who would ever want to seriously threaten Miss

Pike and why? He scratched his arm before collecting himself and scurrying upstairs to join the others and upon the landing and was much relieved to see his mother's face.

'Just slipping downstairs to close all the windows,' she said, her hand trailing down the banisters. 'Hurry the girls for me will you William? I believe they're checking the bedroom windows. I do hope they've done as I asked and not touched anything.'

He gave his mother an assuring smile, neatly slipped past her and headed toward the room echoing with whispers.

The girls' marvelling faces were bathed bright orange from the setting sun outside. Alphonza looked as if she had just discovered the lost ark, for draped over an iron Victorian bedstead, amid the heady aroma of mothballs were the most exquisite gloves, scarves, silk dresses and shawls.

'Oh, William there you are. Look at these clothes. They're absolutely beautiful,' she enthused. 'Look at this dress. It could be from the nineteen fifties. It's stunning!' She held the evening dress against herself and bent down to reach for its hem, fanning the rich dark blue material to reveal a dazzling display of silk embroidered peacock eyes shimmering with gold and silver sequins.

'Are the pair of you crazy?' whispered William. 'These are Miss Pike's personal belongings. You just can't wade through them willy-nilly.'

'Oh, give over,' teased Leigh. 'If the truth be known none of us liked Pike, especially after she threatened to have Nellie put down. Anyway, I've a feeling that Pike won't be coming back.'

'Hats!' shouted Alphonza.

There on a wardrobe, piled up high, was an assortment of round boxes. Suddenly from downstairs came shouts from Mrs Phillips asking for Leigh's help. Grimacing, Leigh plodded from the room.

'Please William, I've never seen clothes as lovely as these. Lets just have a little sneak at the hats,' pleaded Alphonza.

'Oh, all right,' said William, 'but afterwards we must put everything back.'

He stretched on tiptoe to reach for the first pile. Clasping the box at the bottom he began to slide it gently towards him.

'Careful!' shouted Alphonza, her hands reaching out to take the burden of the load, but it was too late. In his haste, William had seized far too many. Swaying vulnerably, the tower of boxes toppled to the ground.

'What's going on up there?' called his mother.

'Nothing,' replied William as Alphonza placed the tips of her fingers to anxious rounded lips. They allowed a moments silence before continuing their explorations. On inspection most of the boxes seemed empty, although Alphonza did manage to find an exquisite feathered cap.

'I wonder if there are any gloves to go with the dress? I can just see them now...long dark blue with sequined veins... Wicked!' She lifted the lid on another box and stopped in dismay. 'Whatever's in here?'

She handed William the box. William pushed the pink tissue aside to see more clearly. His hand then froze. William couldn't believe his eyes, for there amid the strips of delicate paper was another carved wolf pup. He held it up within the room's orange glow. They both looked at it in wonder.

'Come on you two,' shouted Leigh from downstairs. 'Fashion show's over. We've got to go.'

William's heart raced for a moment while he and Alphonza peered questioningly at each other.

'We had better tidy things up William,' said Alphonza, as she made to replace the first of the boxes. William hesitated for a moment before starting to help. Alphonza was just about to replace the carving when he suddenly stopped her.

'No, not the wolf!' he snapped.

'What?' she said startled. 'Why?'

'Because....' He tried to avoid her stare, 'because it's coming with me.'

Alphonza gave William a surprised but cool look.

'That's stealing, William.'

William's face flushed red. He was desperate to tell her everything but recalled Mrs Gardner's words. More shouts came from downstairs.

'In time I will tell you Alphonza, but please trust me when I say this wolf has to come with me.'

Alphonza looked confused. 'I really don't understand William.'

'Look I promise I will explain one day, but for now can I ask for a promise from you, that is, not to tell anyone what I've done, not even Leigh.'

Alphonza looked directly into William's eyes. She felt a deep sincerity about him, a sincerity that required no further questioning. She gave him a small smile and respected his wish. William returned her warmth and buried the pup within his jacket.

Outside it was beginning to get dark. Mrs Phillips realised that in the circumstances it would be safer if her husband were to drive Alphonza home and that everyone should have an early night as they would be having a busy day tomorrow cattle herding. Leigh's face dropped.

'Oh, nightmare of nightmares…not cattle herding. Dad will turn into a wild animal. I'll die…we'll all die. It'll be chaos!'

Alphonza's face lit up.

'Sounds fun. Can I come?'

'Absolutely,' responded Mrs Phillips. 'We need all the help we can get.'

'Wow!' She smiled as they left Miss Pike's house, leaving a dishevelled football on the front lawn.

William sat up in his bed biting his lower lip. He glanced over to the two pups now poised on the mantelpiece. Today had been the weirdest day of his life. He wondered about Miss Pike, would she ever return or had she, like Judith Tench, really disappeared? Why, like Mrs Gardner, did she also have one of the pups? What are these wolves and what was their purpose? Have I really been chosen to solve this mystery, and if so, by whom and why….why, why, why?

There was no way he was going to sleep tonight. Abandoning his bed, he made towards the window and drew back the curtains. The deep blue sky outside sparkled with stars bearing a likeness to the peacock dress that Alphonza had discovered. He could see the leafy branches of an apple tree with the light of a full moon seeping through its branches providing torchlight for the creatures of the night. William suddenly felt a heaving in his chest, a deep yearning to visit the wood. It was dark and he had never been to the woods at night - had he the courage? He needed to find out. The bright moon would light the way.

Having dressed, he slid from his room and amid the heavy snores from his family, crept down stairs, careful to avoid steps that would meanly creak.

Outside in the yard he startled a rat, which in turn startled him. Gripping his nerves he gathered his bike and sped down the drive, the tyres heaving hollow-sounding spits of gravel.

Passing Miss Pike's house he again couldn't help but think of her. Why had she been so mean? She was young once and if those clothes where anything to go by, possibly very glamorous. She had possessions enough but her being mean had cost her dearly, including friendship. No one knew her story fully and as his granddad had always told him, "Everything happens for a reason."

Carried by his own trepidation, William eventually arrived at the borders of the wood, which looked ominous against the deep blue of the sky, like a great black wave ready to engulf anything within its path. Once inside he stepped amongst the looming trees. His senses felt heightened and alert. Was this fear he wondered? It was dark and the deeper he journeyed, the darker it grew. In the stillness of the night the crunch and snap of twigs beneath his feet seemed louder. His breathing became light and tense. What in the hell was he doing? What if he wasn't alone? What if someone or something was in the wood, watching him?

He suddenly felt scared as the trees became more naked and prickly, their lower branches appearing like sinister hands ready to clutch passing souls. William started to feel uncomfortable and suspicious of the wood he so loved, it not only pricking his mind with fear but twisting and teasing him with spiteful thoughts. Just what did he think he was doing, reacting to some ludicrous dreams? But William felt they were a message, a cry for help - a hand reaching out from a desperate void. What was he doing befriending silly old Mrs Gardner? Shouldn't he be with people his own age? But he liked and trusted her, and regardless of her age, felt that they enjoyed a respective understanding. And what was he doing stealing from Miss Pike's house? Felt he had a right, did he? Well, how was he going to explain that to the police?

William drew his fist to his face, shocked. For the first time he felt truly afraid. He couldn't determine fantasy from reality. The wood was now so dark he could barely see. He heard the painful screech of a fox, its cry freezing the very marrow of his being. Above him an owl hooted. He looked up and found its wide eyes staring at him. It swivelled its head then dropped from its branch into the darkness.

William felt alone, alone with fear. He couldn't progress any further. The wood seemed like a monster, all consuming with a smile that stretched grisly and awaiting. He felt the sudden urge to run and without question turned and started to plunge back through the trees. Unseen branches whipped his face and snatched at his clothes. He drew his arms up protectively and as he pushed further on, began to sense an overwhelming presence building from behind, as if he were being followed. Fearful, he glanced round and thought he saw something move in the blackness. A branch snapped. The sound was deep and heavy. He began to sweat. In the distance he thought he heard another cry, but this was no fox. He heard it again. This time he felt it not to be a cry, but a howl, a faint long howl, like that which some believe a wolf makes before it makes chase. He shivered and hurried further through the undergrowth. The crunch of the wood beneath his feet seemed horrendous but he didn't care, he had to get out. Whatever it was behind him was getting closer. He thought he could hear breathing, which seemed to heave louder and louder, faster and faster. He could feel his blood pump within his head, forcing a heavy pressure in his ears. It was no good, he would have to face whatever it was. With clenched fists he swung round and shouted, 'No!'

But there was nothing, nothing but the stillness of the night. As he dropped his chin to his chest William knew that he had confronted his first enemy - himself.

Reaching the barbed wire fence, he stretched under it and stumbled gratefully into the open field.

William now felt a little clearer regarding the wolves. He would allow things to happen and play his role as best he could. It was then that he noticed a small pair of eyes shining in the depths of the grass. He quickened towards them but they vanished out of sight. He heard movement near to his side. There they were again. He fell to his knees to be at their level and with his arms outstretched, gently pushed the grass either side. There, to his surprise, was Nellie. The snappy little dog that everyone was so familiar with, seemed calm and collected. About her was a knowing serenity, revealing something he'd never seen. William stroked her coat. It felt cool in the night air.

'I do love you Nellie, we all do.' Within the tranquillity of the night, William observed the peace that Nellie had with nature. It was time to go home.

They had just passed into the narrow stone track that led to the fields before the wood when William noticed some house lights flickering through the hedge at his side. Huntly Roach, the woodland's neighbour, was still up, whiling away the early hours with his love for gambling.

Bill Phillips rented the fields around Great Cheriton wood from Huntly Roach, who had only purchased them from a previous owner the previous year. Almost doubling the rent as soon as he could, pinching Bill's already ailing business even further.

Walking past the entrance to the house William suddenly noticed Marcus Price's vehicle in the drive. Intrigued, he stopped to look and could hear the sound of raucous laughter coming from within. William drew himself up behind the safety of the vehicle while

Nellie busied herself smelling the fragrance on its wheels. He could see that the lights came from two windows. One from upstairs, revealing what looked like a landing. The other from the dinning room downstairs, where either side of an enormous polished table sat Huntly Roach and Price himself. The two men were playing cards. Roach's fat, ruddy face puffed anxiously away on a large cigar, whilst he scrutinised his hand. Price peered at him above his hand with a smug grin. Positioned in the middle of the table was a large, green, velvet jewel wrap, bound with ribbon.

Upstairs, the diminutive figure of Huntly's wife, Sandy, appeared, looking somewhat vexed as she began to open the compartments of a tall chest of drawers, searching frantically beneath layers of stored linen.

Downstairs, Huntly's face creased tight as he placed what he knew to be a weak card on the table. Price, arching an eyebrow, pulled a card smugly from his own hand and let it fall, his grin contorting and cracking into hard laughter. He pulled the prized green wrap to himself and held it with a smooth glee.

Upstairs, Sandy tossed a handful of linen to the floor and marched stiffly out of sight.

Downstairs William could see words exchanged within the smoky room while Price poured whisky into two small tumblers, downing his in one. Both men then rose from their chairs and shook hands. Huntly Roach then disappeared from view with Price following.

Suddenly, the front door of the house clicked open. Panic hit William. He couldn't run down the drive, he would be seen. Where could he hide? He had to think quickly. In the shadows of the lawn he could see a crude statue of a Roman gladiator. Hunching down like a crab, he sidled towards it and took cover behind it. Where was Nellie?

'Nellie,' whispered William. From the shadows her curious black and white face appeared. She trotted to him and he hugged her behind the statue as Price and Roach stepped into the drive.

'Bad luck Huntly,' said Price, holding up the green wrap. 'I hope your dear wife, Sandy, doesn't notice it's missing.'

Roach puffed on his cigar.

'I'll challenge you for it back one of these days and win. You'll see!'

Price shaking his head laughed while slipping into his vehicle and with a broad smile, manoeuvred out of the drive. All the excitement was too much for Nellie and she let out a small pine. Alarmed, Roach looked out across the lawn.

'Who's there?'

William thought of Mrs Gardner's, "hold fast," as he and Nellie shrank behind the statue. Roach, scowling, puffed on the cigar then turned to retire inside where his dear wife, Sandy, arms folded, was waiting.

Chapter 5

Chaos

The awakening shouts at the bottom of the stairs just about reached William's drowsy ears. With an effort he was able to answer the call with an audible grunt. He then removed himself lightly from his bed and started to dress in a dreamlike state, realising minutes later that he *was* dreaming, and that his sluggish figure still lay beneath the duvet. Ashamed, he bolted from the bed and with the speed of an ant drew on his clothes.

The farm's backyard was a rambling affair. Many of the buildings were in need of repair, especially the old stables, whose walls were covered in lichen and even tufts of grass growing between the stonework. The end stable had become a temporary enclosure for Nellie who was not aloud to take part in cattle herding, for she grew too excitable and once nearly caused a fatal accident. Remembering her calmness in the night, William couldn't help but take a peek at the dog, with which he believed he'd carved a new friendship. But upon opening the top half of a stable door, he found only the rebellious Nellie he'd always known, furious she was being forbidden the joys of the rodeo.

'Don't let trouble out!' hollered Bill Phillips.

William turned to see his father delivering his instructions in the belly of the yard. Circled around him were Leigh and his mother, accompanied by a wide-eyed Alphonza and a rather rough looking Tommy Andrews, who had seen another late pub night at the Half Moon. After apologising to Nellie, William closed the door and made to join them, just as his father was handing out sticks for protection. Alphonza looked most concerned as she reached for hers. Noticing, William offered assurance.

'Don't be scared. They won't attack you,' he said. 'But they might need a little encouragement along the trail.'

'Mine's a special stick,' said Leigh, butting in. 'Dad says I can keep it to help those who have trouble getting out of bed.'

William raised his stick playfully at her in a mock sword fight. Leigh immediately parried him off and ran to the gate were the expectant cattle were waiting.

'Allow me to introduce Smash,' she said, clambering onto the gate and reaching out to stroke a young heifer. Alphonza, not used to farm animals, decided to keep her distance. The sight of the restless cattle frightened her and the stick that she now held tight gave little comfort.

'Do they bite?' she asked.

'No,' replied William laughing, also jumping onto the gate and hugging the heifer's head. 'Smash is quite friendly, a sensitive soul at heart and very bright…she trusts us. Dad's going to keep her on as a milker.'

Alphonza stepped forward and from a safe distance petted Smash's ears. The heifer, although unusually twitchy, bucked playfully. At that moment, the screech of a vehicle's tyres could be heard and the youngsters turned to see the Land Rover reverse into the yard.

'All aboard,' shouted Bill Phillips.

While Mrs Phillips made for the passenger seat, everyone else climbed into the back; gripping the canvas free frame and peering over the driver's roof as the vehicle sped off down the farm track. The cattle would be travelling all the way through the village until they reached the Half Moon pub, beside which lay a track leading to new pastures. It was vital, however, that all other road entrances and vulnerable homes were guarded and that the cattle were steered appropriately along the correct route.

Upon the Land Rover's return, William was the last to be dropped, guarding the road left at the bottom of the farm drive. Resting his stick across his shoulders, he watched the vehicle speed back up the farm track to release the cattle. The drone of the engine gone, William for a moment savoured the peace around him. The faint song of a skylark teased the air, instilling in him a great sense of gratitude. How wonderful nature is and how fortunate he was to experience it so intimately. He peered over a bramble hedge where he could see Miss Pike's house, as always the curtains semi drawn. It was then, while waiting, that he felt an urge to peep through the kitchen window. The cattle had not yet broached the drive - he had time. Scrambling through a track that Nellie had worn, he ran to the house and peeped within. To gain a possible view of the pantry, he pressed his face tight against the kitchen window, but the angle gave him nothing. Disappointed he turned and moved away, unaware of a shifty hand that had pinched back a curtain to see.

William was about to scramble through the hedge when he heard a light click. His head twisted sharply and his eyes were drawn to the front door. Was that the sound of its lock, he wondered, or the door's wood shrinking in the heat? Intrigued, he went to find out, when suddenly, a distant rumble whirred through his ears and the scrape and grind of hooves began to thump along the farm track - the rodeo had begun.

As William ran back to guard the left side of the road, a sudden feeling of dread seeped through his veins. Looking up the track, he could see the herd approaching, their heads heaving wild and determined. It was an image that made him shiver. It reminded him of the wolves. As the cattle exploded into the road, William threw out his arms, steering them right until all twenty beasts had bustled passed him, leaving a cloud of dust behind. The Land Rover, bringing up the rear, then screeched to a halt.

'Leap in boy,' bellowed his father.

Without hesitation William threw himself on board, just as the vehicle sped off. Cattle herding made his father very tense, anyone who helped had to have their wits about them at all times.

At the bottom of the road William's mother was guarding a lane entrance. Ignoring her, the cattle plunged on to investigate the cluster of homes ahead. Granny Phillips, who resided in one, was out patrolling her driveway with her obligatory broom. Opposite her, guarding another driveway was Alphonza. The zealous cattle swelled between them, and intrigued by the matrix of possible entrances, drew to a halt. Alphonza, realising that there was absolutely nothing between her and the excited beasts was suddenly hit with panic. Her body tensed straight and she cast a sharp glance at Granny Phillips, who was brandishing her broom and hollering like some Celtic warrior woman. Inspired, Alphonza flung out her arms challenging the beasts with her stick. Startled, the animals hurled their heads up and charged on, heading towards a major fork in the road, the trickiest place on the entire trail.

With arms ablaze, Leigh guarded the main road travelling left. Before her, Tommy was holding up the herd so the Land Rover could pass into the right hand lane with those on board to cover more vulnerable spots. Tensions were mounting, however, for due to a high, protruding garden wall, the road was rendered narrow making it very testing indeed. The steaming cattle began to huddle up in a frenzied scrum. Matters only grew worse with the sudden build up of motorists either end. At the front the animals were growing increasingly restless. Barking like a dog to hold them back, Tommy Andrew's neck and face were turning beetroot-red as motorists' started to sound their horns.

'I say there,' a man bawled at Granny Phillips from an open top sports car. 'Can't you put those creatures on a lead or something.'

Granny, indignant, turned.

'And I say as well...up yours you toffy nosed fathead!'

The man shot back into his seat and revved his car on, tooting furiously. With the heat of the sun glaring down, the situation was beginning to swell like a tender boil about to burst. The cattle were now thrown into a state of confusion. At one end was Tommy, at the other the man in the open top sports car, and engulfed by cattle between the two, the Land Rover.

With her trust bullied, Smash couldn't tolerate anymore. Head bucking, she pushed her way through. Trotting gallantly past Tommy Andrews with head down, she charged towards Leigh. Without haste, Leigh hurled herself onto the side of the road. Roused by their leader, the others followed, breaking the intended rodeo path like rowdy youths and causing a stampede down the wrong route.

Horrified shouts and screams came from the Land Rover as everyone looked on in shock. Hooking her broom beneath the back of the vehicle's frame and with an enormous surge of adrenaline, Granny Phillips heaved herself onboard, ripping her skirt in the process.

'Crikey,' she puffed, 'I think I've ruptured me undies!'

A desperate Tommy Andrews and Leigh catapulted themselves onboard, before the Land Rover accelerated off in pursuit of the rampaging herd, which due to a decent in the road had gathered velocity.

A toothy, bespectacled girl was driving up the hill in a bright red Mini. In the passenger seat was a portly man who, face buried in a book, was testing her on the Highway Code.

'Now, Amber,' he posed, 'in the event of an emergency stop, which appliances should be used simultaneously?'

Amber did not answer. Surprised, the man asked again. 'Amber, in the event of an emergency stop which…' Before he could finish, Amber let out a wrenching scream as the entourage of animals bore down on her car like a tidal surge.

'Amber,' shouted the man. 'Emergency stop, *now*!'

The hurtling wave of cattle parted like the Red Sea, swallowing the girl's car in a torrent of excitement as they pressed on down the road, the Land Rover racing like a mad carnival exhibit behind. Granny Phillips, clutching desperately onto the framework, pleaded to Bill that he was driving too fast.

'Close your eyes then,' implored William.

'Certainly not,' she snapped. 'I want to be able to see when I get killed!'

Alphonza looked on in shock, not knowing whether to laugh or cry as Leigh shrugged her shoulders and gestured mockingly towards the sky with a pleading smile as the Land Rover sped on.

The first, unguarded house was none other than the vicarage itself. The gates were wide open for any welcome visitors. As luck would have it for the Reverend, Smash and her crew sailed straight past. All accept Betty, that is, the slowest of the herd, who trailing at the far end, couldn't help but notice the lovely nasturtium flowers creeping over a rockery in the centre of the lawn. Abandoning the others, she sauntered through the inviting gates towards the lush blooms.

The Reverend Gillespie was sitting in his study, his back to the window. He was entertaining the Reverend Rugby, a short, stocky man with wavy black hair, with one of his many uneventful jokes. He was about to deliver the punch line. '….and the Pilgrim took the bag, looked inside and do you know what he found?' said the Reverend Gillespie, about to collapse into barrels of laughter.

'A cow,' shouted the Reverend Rugby.

Reverend Gillespie giggled.

'Nice try Rugby, but no, he found a ….'

'Good grief.' shouted the Reverend Rugby. 'Since when have your sermons extended to farm animals?'

By this point Betty was peering through the study window. The Reverend Gillespie turned to face a window steamed up with Betty's breath, a flower dribbling from her mouth.

'Good God! I've beasts in my garden!' cried the Reverend, running hysterically from his study with Rugby tiptoeing behind. Both men bolted into the drive, the Reverend Gillespie, a flurry of arms, chasing Betty from his horticultural Eden. Flying from the passenger seat of the Land Rover, thoroughly embarrassed, Jackie Phillips offered humble apologies. The Reverend Gillespie clasped his hands beneath his chin.

'Mrs Phillips,' he postulated, 'God's work is never done.'

The Reverend Rugby, smirking, broke into fits of rasping giggles behind.

Toot toots, came from the Land Rover, suggesting that should Jackie leap in 'sharpish,' for Betty was already up marching with the rest of the herd who were now thundering towards the house of Marcus Price.

'Alphonza, your mobile,' shouted William. 'Isn't your mum cleaning today? Tell her to shut the gates or something…quick!'

Alphonza wrestled inside the pocket of her jeans. Finding her mobile she called her mother, who could barely hear a thing amid the noise of the motoring vehicle, but managed to ascertain instructions to shut the gates. A considerable wake of traffic was beginning to build up behind them.

'Oh, dignity, dignity,' wailed Granny Phillips. 'Where art thou gone? Thou hath left me for sure.'

Having tossed her feather duster to one side, Rosie Pink assembled herself hastily in the Price's splendid drive. She suddenly remembered that the tall iron gates were electronically controlled. In the distance she could hear an awesome rumble and looked up to see a scrum of bobbing heads and nostrils flaring. Like her daughter, this was a first for her. Rosie shook her head from a momentary state of paralysis and plunged towards the open garage in search of the gate's controls. Eyes frantically scanning the walls, her hand reached for an obvious switch. Flicking it up she glanced towards the gates with expectation. There was no movement. She then heard a kick and a rumble and looked up to see the garage door starting to drop. Bending awkwardly, she struggled to get out but the movement of the overhanging door was too swift. Before she knew it, she was trapped.

The thick of the heard surged past the gates towards the open road. All but Smash, that is, whose inquisitive nature felt drawn toward the lavish house.

In the dark, with outstretched hands, Rosie felt her way to the garage's side door. Discovering the lock, with relief she immediately opened it only to be met with Smash's wide-eyed glare. Rosie froze.

'Honey, you have my absolute respect!' she trembled and slammed the door shut.

But Smash's curiosity had been drawn yet again, this time by the sight of an open side door.

Act Two of Tchaikovsky's Swan Lake had just been placed onto a music deck. Its entrancing opening bars lying sweet upon Smash's ears. She ambled her way through a small passageway and found herself within a decorative kitchen, its tall ceiling strewn with copper pots and pans. Smash sniffed the air, her body tensed and a fearful shiver ran through her. She then followed her nose through a tall door that led into a grand reception hall. Her black and white coat matched the tiles of the polished floor and an elaborate chandelier high above sparkled diamond dots on her quivering back. It was then that her attention was drawn to an emoting figure, all in black, within an adjacent room. Smash peered through an open mahogany door to observe further.

Totally unaware of her visitor, Chrystal Price continued to dance with passion, her blonde ponytail dropping in time with the music as her svelte figure embraced the full beauty of its score.

Smash withdrew her head from the room only to turn and face a horrified William who had followed her trail. Their eyes locked in a fixed stare, the moment being held just a little to long for William to feel it normal. Gently, he stepped forward and reached toward her, but Smash tossed her head and started to survey the hall's wide and elegant twisting staircase. Before William could do anything, she began to ascend the stairs. The heavy framed paintings hanging against the panelled walls, trembled with each weighty step. As the music travelled up, so did Smash. Up and up she ventured, her eyes wide and determined. Heart thumping, William watched, baffled.

Suddenly, Smash halted in her tracks. Standing absolutely still for a moment, she sniffed the air and drew her ears back. Something had made her nervous, something strange and menacing. She then peered over the banister at William, who was staring up at her astonished. Again their eyes seemed to lock as if the animal were trying to communicate something, something that animals have the capacity to feel. She then jostled her head and turned, and with unprecedented speed bustled her way back down the stairs, her big bottom banging against the wall and bouncing onto the banister as she rounded the corners.

William dashed to the front door and swiftly unbolted it, withdrawing himself back to guide Smash out, just as Rosie stepped into the hall. Stunned, Rosie threw her hands to her mouth as she watched Smash, tail flicking wildly, find her escape, William herding behind. Hearing a light 'ching', Rosie stared aghast as a final whip of the tail caught a decorative vase. As it swayed teasingly, Rosie threw herself towards it, the vase thankfully coming to an appreciated standstill in time with the music, which had drawn to its haunting conclusion.

Chrystal Price sprang dramatically from the living room, arms held high as Rosie rolled over onto all fours pretending to flick cobwebs from beneath a table.

'Oh, Rosie. I could cry, yes, I could cry…that act gets me every time. Tchaikovsky - what a man. I say Rosie, shall we be really naughty and fix ourselves a small gin and tonic? How about it sweetie?' Rosie, without hesitation, gave a firm nod.

Outside, everyone's mouths were held agape as they witnessed Smash departing via the front door.

'Now that's what I call leaving in style,' quipped Leigh.

William chased her on with the rest of the herd, which had stopped to feast on the roadside's lush grass. It wasn't long before they'd had enough, however, and were stampeding again, Smash hustling her way to the front and marching towards a busy crossroads.

Hearts were really in mouths now as everyone could clearly see the horrendous throb of holiday traffic, pouring like the sweat from their brows. Bill Phillips had no choice but to keep driving, his face full of disbelief, whilst Jackie buried hers in her hands. Those in the back held their breaths in anticipation of the disaster that loom ahead.

Then something happened, something miraculous. From the hot quivering mirage before them, a strange sphere of light seemed to appear, its rays dropping and stretching into a lean willowy form. William watched in wonder as its human like frame started to move nobly towards the approaching herd, stopping in line with a narrow lane that led off to the right. Branching out unusually long arms, the figure ceremoniously brought the rebellious cattle to a standstill. Oblivious to the intense heat, a nervous shiver ran down William's spine. The figure, now clearly that of an elderly man, motioned slowly towards the adjacent lane With each broad step, his long white hair lifted and rested on the back of his green attire. The cattle, one by one, Smash leading, calmly followed the man as he paced his way lightly down the lane, the mesmerised parade of animals passing all open driveways without interest. The Land Rover chugged behind, gratefully releasing the tense queue of traffic at its rear.

The Half Moon pub, a sight for sore eyes, eventually appeared. The mysterious man strode past its welcoming door and broached the stony track that led to the lush pastures of the twenty-two acre field. William noticed the man seemed not to touch the gate, as with ease it swung open. The entranced animals spilled magically inside, skipping and jumping with joy into the vast open field, like children released from school.

Everyone accept Granny, who was escorted down by Tommy, leapt from the now stationary vehicle, throwing themselves with great relief into the comfort of the fresh long grass. Leigh stole a glance at Alphonza, whose face was still in shock. For a moment all were silent, staring appreciatively into the cool blue of the sky.

'We owe everything to that man,' announced William, catching his breath.

'What man? asked his mother surprised.

'*That* man,' insisted William.

There was a silence that was suddenly smothered in a baffled chorus of 'what and who?'

His face pale, William stood up and before explaining himself further, rushed to the gate. Peering down the narrow track, he saw no one. As strangely as he'd appeared, the mysterious man had vanished.

Chapter 6

Guardians

Later, with the intense heat of the day lifted, William offered to take what his parents had assembled as a humble apology to the Gillespie's.

With the sunlight softened, he decided to make the trek on foot. Passing Miss Pike's house, with the day's events swirling strangely within his conscience, he began to feel light headed. All through the day he'd been thinking of the Mysterious Man and couldn't understand why no one else had seen him. He'd even looked through his mother's medical book hoping to better understand the symptoms of hallucination, but it only confused him further. Reaching the bottom of the road he shrugged from his wonder and called in at his granny's to collect a bottle of sherry, which she knew the Reverend was partial to. Having placed it carefully in a cardboard box, already bulging with home made bread, eggs, lettuce and other goodies from the farm, he continued his journey.

The vicarage held a tranquil calm, a calm that was broken by William's strident rap on the door. William was soon greeted by the scent of oranges and polish, a familiar smell that the vicarage's interior always seemed to bear. The Reverend smiled graciously at the offering, especially the sherry.

'Splendid dear boy, splendid,' he whispered, as he placed the bottle behind a wooden settle in the hall. 'What the eye can't see, the mouth can't criticize. Do thank your granny on my behalf …and your parents of course.'

William grinned as the Reverend trundled out the back to call for his wife.

'Darling, young William Phillips is here with produce from his farm. Splendid, what?'

At the bottom of a patch of wilderness the tall tweed figure of Mrs Gillespie, swathed in a huge netted hat was dangling over a beehive.

'Oh, rather Darling, rather,' she snorted as she made to grip the hives side. 'Fix young William up with the appropriate garments will you, I'm sure he'd like a peep at the bees.'

The Reverend Gillespie decked William up in a very big-netted hat, beneath which he was barely visible. Dispatching him at a safe distance from the hives, the Reverend then waved him off and like a giant jelly-fish, floated down toward the humming apiary.

Mrs Gillespie's tweed skirt pinched round her knee's as she readied herself to remove the upper half of the hive.

'Don't be frightened young William, like most creatures bees can sense fear. Remain calm and you shan't get stung.'

William gulped, as with a hollow bump, Mrs Gillespie withdrew the lid, her toothy face beaming beneath her veil. Within seconds the area around them was flooded with a cloud of startled bees.

'Oh, marvellous William, marvellous,' hooted Mrs Gillespie peering in. 'See how the combs are forming? They're almost dripping with honey. How absolutely yummy.'

Leaning to look, William could see the heavily dappled combs around which the bees were weaving. The hives musty smell pervaded their protective nets, and for a moment they both savoured the summer jewel before them.

Suddenly, as if prompted by something unseen, the bee's lifted from the hive, swarming in alarmed circles around their visitors.

'What!' quivered Mrs Gillespie. 'This is not their usual practice, not their usual practice at all. Something's not right, William.' She replaced the hive's top with a soft clump. By this point the agitated bees began to swarm on mass around them, the very sight alarming the Reverend.

'Darling!' he gasped, hurling himself from his garden chair. 'What's got into the bees? I've never scene them behave like this.'

'There upset!' piped Mrs Gillespie. 'For some unknown reason, darling, the bees are upset. Remain calm William. We'll take respective action when they settle.'

But the bees didn't settle. Instead they continued to swarm, their whirling mass thickening. Suddenly, with unprecedented force, they shot off, flying directly toward the vicarage. Horrified, the Reverend Gillespie squatted on the ground, but the bees had no intention of attacking him. Instead they rose up and spun round in a huge circle before dropping like a squadron of planes toward one of the upper windows, aiming with precision at its open frame.

'Their going inside,' exclaimed a disbelieving William.

'It's incredible!' marvelled Mrs Gillespie. I've never seen anything like it, ever!'

The bees continued to swoop through the window. Some of them crashed into the glass above, only to redouble their efforts and dive in again. The Reverend Gillespie, mouth agape, rose from the lawn. Suddenly, a horrific scream bellowed from the house followed by thuds and bumps.

'Good God!' gasped Mrs Gillespie. *Someone* is upstairs.'

William threw his netted hat to the ground and ran to the vicarage, the Reverend stumbling after.

As he approached the hall he heard the sound of feet tumbling down the stairs.

'Hey,' shouted William, but before he could see who it was, the settle in the hall was tossed from the wall, interrupting William's view of the fleeing figure. The rectory door then slammed shut and William just managed to glimpse through the stained-glass windows at its side, the flash of a denim jacket.

The startled Gillespie's soon assembled in the hall, where a number of bees were now hovering.

'A burglar for sure. How dreadful!' announced Mrs Gillespie, her hair dangling messily over her face.

The Reverend ventured upstairs to inspect the room, while a wide-eyed William turned to face Mrs Gillespie.

'It was incredible. It was as if the bees were flushing the burglar out. Protecting you…or something you have.'

Mrs Gillespie looked thoughtful.

'Those bees, what darlings they are.'

Hearing the soft steps of the Reverend coming down the stairs, they both looked up.

'Well,' he started, clearing his throat, 'nothing seems to be damaged or taken, for that matter. Most baffling!'

Mrs Gillespie was correcting herself somewhat oddly in the mirror.

'Darling, we shall have to notify the police. Dreadful, how absolutely dreadful!' She then noticed the bottle of sherry perched up against the wall. 'Dash it, look…a bottle of sherry. I don't remember leaving that there, do you darling?'

The Reverend Gillespie stuck his hands into his pockets and shrugged innocence.

William smiled, not just at the sherry but the way the Gillespie's seemed so unperturbed. In fact William felt more shaken than they. First the cattle, and now the bees. What had provoked them to react so strangely? He thought of the twisting staircase in the Courthouse. What had Smash sensed there? The 'get out room' perhaps? As he helped the Gillespie's replace the settle, his mind dizzied with the possibilities. The wood beneath his grip felt grainy and old. For some reason it made him think again of the mysterious man. William wondered if he would be seeing him again.

Chapter 7

Risks

Tuesday morning. As the weather, thankfully, had not yet broke, Bill Phillips thought it wise to push on with preparations necessary for baling the field next to Great Cheriton Wood. Having cut the grass the previous afternoon, it required turning in order to dry out the immature hay sufficiently. Tommy Andrews, who preferred tractors to cattle, was out in the back yard along with Bill fiddling with the necessary machinery. Nellie sat with interest beside them, her head occasionally tilting to peep at the swallows swooping skilfully into the shelter of an empty barn. Any day now their young would be leaving their nests.

Jackie Phillips, calling and waving from the farmhouse, was off to town for the obligatory weekly shopping. Leigh and William were going with her.

Reflecting on yesterday's adventure, Mrs Phillips was conscious of the state of the road, which indeed did look messy, especially before the nightmarish fork where Granny lived. William and Leigh giggled seeing Granny's vain attempts to clear the cow muck, creating quite an artistic picture of swirls and whirls from the strokes of her broom. Jackie Phillips laughed to herself whilst picturing in her mind Granny receiving some great accolade for contemporary art.

Luckily, Mrs Phillips found an easy space to park in the town centre, right by the clock. William liked the town. If the mood was right, aided perhaps by the sound of passing gulls, the rows of white, pink and blue washed buildings, almost led him to believe he was by the sea.

After deliberating how long they might be, everyone decided they would return to the car at half past eleven and headed off in their chosen direction. William immediately made for his favourite shop, The Green Dragon, which was a real Aladdin's cave of antiques and collectables. The window display this week was amazing, for suspended from a rail amidst gramophones, teddy bears, clocks and sci-fi memorabilia were an assortment of eye catching, colourful string puppets. There was a King and his Queen, a wizard, and a thick-lipped mediaeval giant. Next to him hung a red-cheeked policeman and farmer, whilst alongside these was a glazed looking Red Riding Hood. William couldn't help but notice with wonder the character hung next to her - a wolf.

All were poised quite still in their hypnotic suspension as if eerily awaiting animation. William's enjoyment of the display was soon interrupted by the arrival of a girl bearing a stool. Placing it as close to the window as possible, she clambered onto it and reached up to unhook the wolf from the rail.

William quickly curtailed any disappointment from his mind and entered the shop to feast his eyes upon more of its treasures. By the door was a 1940's radio emitting the gentle sound of a piano. William wandered down the main isle, marvelling at the quaint toys and bric-a-brac from times gone by, lit spookily by the sunlight from outside. He was quite surprised on arriving at the shop's counter to find Sterling Price, Marcus's son. He was a well kept but introverted boy who had his father's dark hair, trimmed neatly with a straight-cut fringe. Before him on the counter was the wolf puppet. It was being wrapped in tissue.

'Hello, Sterling,' said William.

Sterling turned, startled, his pale complexion turning red.

'Oh, hello. You're the Phillips boy aren't you,' he replied with a clipped tone, his eyes dropping to the floor.

'Yes, we met at the woodland meeting,' said William, watching Sterling hurriedly pack his purchase into his bag. 'That's a lovely puppet you have there.'

'Oh, yes…it…um…is.' Sterling was stumbling over his words. 'It's, for my cousin.'

William knew that he was fibbing.

'Me and my sister have a string puppet each, just like the ones in the window.'

Sterling's face lit up.

'Oh really? Which ones?'

'Well,' replied William, 'I've a pirate and she's a clown.'

'Are you saying she has a clown or that she is one?'

William was slightly taken aback by Sterling's sudden aloof manner.

'She *has* a clown. Sorry, I'm not as well schooled as you.'

'My father tells me not to mix with the peasants.'

'And just who are the peasants?' asked William, knowing full well who he was referring to.

Sterling looked down, embarrassed.

'You won't tell anyone will you Phillips?'

'About what?' asked William.

'About the puppets.'

'Why should I?' said William, astonished.

Sterling sniffed a reluctant smile, clutched the bag to himself and left.

Outside in the street William could see his mother in the charity shop foraging for bargains. Time would soon be running out so he quickly upped his pace to explore the gallery lower down.

Gallery Garnish was an impressive shop, full of local artists' work, as well as those from farther afield. Looking through the window, William was particularly intrigued with an oil painting of a naked man huddled in the corner of a brown, bare walled room. On his head was a crown of coins. The man's expression was one of sadness, possibly unhappy with the burden on his head, thought William.

William had to ring a buzzer in order to be admitted inside. Through the glass he could see Livia Tench, the gallery's curator, release the door with a reluctant air. He wondered if she had received any news about her missing mother Judith. He was dying to ask but couldn't muster the courage.

Livia was dressed in a hugging pinstripe suit, which she looked practically corseted in. Her heavily mascara-lashed eyes shot a hawk-like glance at William.

'You're not to touch a thing!' she rasped. 'And don't stand to close to the paintings, your breath might affect the medium.'

Feeling uncomfortable, William slid behind a pillar to view a sculpture of a classic female figurine sitting royally on a chaise, titled, 'Cassiopeia.' The figure was admiring herself vainly in an ornate hand mirror. Thankfully the trill of a telephone soon broke the awkward silence.

'Hello, Gallery Garnish,' husked Livia. 'Well, hello there stranger. I've got a little pressie for you…Oh, yes, I found it all right…it's in my hand right now.'

Curious, William looked into the ornate mirror into which Cassiopeia gazed, where he could see a reflection of Livia. There, to his disbelief, entwined within her painted nails was a carved wolf pup. William's body shook with nervous excitement.

'Of course, everything costs darling and I did like that ring so much, although not as much as your promise.'

At that moment the door buzzed.

'Look darling, I've a customer, I'll call you later.' She slammed the phone down, placed the wolf beneath her desk and hit the button to release the door. 'I thought I told you not to call into the gallery.'

A young roguish looking man wearing scruffy denim sauntered towards Livia. Sitting on the end of her desk, he teased her chin with his forefinger then rested his hand on his thigh. William again slunk behind the pillar - Troy Cruickshank was someone he didn't want to be noted by.

'So tell me Sexy?' said Troy, his eyes sliding towards Livia's desk draw, 'you've something in there worth a bob or two, eh?'

Livia's eyebrow arched shrewdly.

'Nothing that you'd need concern yourself with Troy, darling.'

Troy leaned over, his hand creeping along to the rear of the desk. Livia quickly raised hers and slapped Troy's wrist hard.

'Didn't you know that curiosity killed the cat!' she whipped, as she removed the wolf from the draw. Her high-heeled shoes clipped hard on the gallery's stone floor as she dropped down some steps to place the wolf within the safety of the cellar, only to find upon her return, Troy at the top of the cellar steps leaning suggestively against the door. Ignoring his flirtations she pushed past him to adjust an ornament in the window. His eager narrow eyes followed her, he then strode behind and ran his finger up the shallow of her back.

'You're a real liberty taker, you are Troy Cruickshank,' groaned Livia, as she circumspectly checked the window.

William seized the opportunity and shot crazily towards the gallery's rear door, jumped down its plummeting steps and hid within the cellar beneath. There on a top shelf was the third wolf pup, but what was he to do now, steal it? He heard the clip of Livia's heels on the steps. Startled, he quickly took cover behind some standing shelves at the back. Peering through them he could see Livia running her fingers through Troy's messy dark hair while he motioned to kiss her rich red lips. William, frightened of being seen, tried to slink back further into the shadows. In doing so, he kicked a plastic bucket in the corner beside him, arousing Livia's attention.

'What was that?' she asked, alarmed.

Troy drew away from her and entered the cellar, while William in the hope of not being discovered huddled himself tight. Troy, sharp-eyed, searched the cellar's rear.

'I can see nothing. Probably rats,' he claimed, his eyes then catching sight of the wolf. He then walked calculatingly backwards until he was level with it, and like a shark, snatched it from the shelf, and hid it beneath the breast of his denim jacket.

'Buzz, buzz, buzz,' went the gallery's front door. Livia straightened herself up and raced for the button to allow a large party of people entrance, enabling Troy to slyly half zip up his jacket. Clutching the handle of the cellar door he slammed it shut. William heard the hard sound of a bolt being drawn across. His heart sunk rapidly - he was trapped.

Chapter 8

Trust

Within the darkness of the cellar, William was met with the claustrophobic sound of nothingness. The cellar door was so thick he couldn't even hear Livia's voice beyond. Should he wait by the opening and burst thuggishly out to freedom, escaping not only surrender but also the burden of having to explain himself? What if Livia recognised him and informed the police, resulting in shame for himself and embarrassment for his family? With shoulders hunched, elbows tight to his belly, his tentative hands searched the blackness about him. Not being able to see his watch, he began to panic - it must be well after eleven thirty. Leigh and his mother would be getting worried. He kicked something soft and could feel the playful texture of bubble wrap. His anxious mind made him move on, resisting the temptation to pinch the tiny cushions and snap them free of air.

The damp musty smell of the cellar felt heavy on his lungs and he started to fear he might be trapped there all night. Perhaps tomorrow, Livia would find a crumpled, suffocated body lying on the floor. His fantasies were soon chased away by a sudden nasty bump to his forehead. William reached up to still a vulnerable, hanging bucket. Carefully he lowered his arms to search for a safe place to rest. Clipping his toe on what seemed to be a stone step, William sank to inspect it further. Feeling a spacious seat he relieved his legs of their weight to contemplate his next move. He wondered about the wolf pup and why Troy Cruickshank should show such an interest in it. Were the carvings known to be valuable and why was the necessity to have them himself growing more intense? He lent back to rest his shoulders, only to find nothing more solid at his back than a thick curtain, which he fell unnervingly through.

Gathering himself together, he could feel two walls either side of him. Standing, he nearly banged his head on a low alcove ceiling. William realised he was in some kind of passageway. He started to feel his way forward and it wasn't long before his toe felt another stone step. Slowly he started to ascend what seemed like a narrow stairway. On reaching its precipice he discovered something panelled with wood before him, a door. But to where? Hopeful, William felt for a latch but there was nothing. Disappointed, he sat back on the steps. Maybe he could hide here and wait for the opportunity of Livia leaving the cellar door open. If the gallery was full of customers he could sneak out undetected. He laughed to himself. Maybe he could shout, "abracadabra," and turn himself into a tiny mouse. Only then, of course, he would risk actually being killed by Livia.

From behind him he suddenly heard a bump and a creak. Startled, he turned to face the door. The bump came again, followed by the creak. He heard the sound of masonry particles falling to the ground, its dust invading his nostrils. William sneezed wildly as the door before him gave one long eerie creak as it miraculously opened.

With a mixture of fearful astonishment and curiosity he ventured through. He felt more steps. Reaching the bottom he stood up. He was still in blackness but stretching his arms wide he sensed he was in some kind of tunnel. The walls felt damp and old. Had this been here a long time, he wondered? He then recollected hearing a story about some old tunnels that ran beneath the town, once used by the gentry and clergy as a form of escape from invaders. Again feeling his way he started to venture down the tunnel, upping his pace as his confidence grew. After some distance the darkness began to bear a dim light enabling him to really quicken his steps. The light grew stronger as he hastened towards it, until eventually he arrived at its source. Looking up he could see a thick heavy iron grid encrusted in rust, beyond it the sky, landscaped with beech trees. Hearing the cackle of rooks within their canopies, he knew instantly that he was beneath the church.

William ventured a little further and could see that the tunnel came to what looked like an abrupt end. But then there was another door. He tried it but it was also locked. He wondered if it, too, would magically open. He then heard an earthy tear and suddenly felt cold dirt trickle down his back. Alarmed, he peered up through the grid and was surprised to see frail twig-like hands pulling it gently away. Beyond these was an old, deeply grained face. With incredible ease the heavy iron grid lifted, and before William could stagger fearfully back, a long arm reached down offering a graceful hand.

'Come,' came a resonant voice.

William boldly took it and was lifted up into the emerging daylight. He was now in full view of his saviour and recognised him immediately as the willowy mysterious man who had rescued his father's cattle the previous day. William for a moment peered transfixed by the old man's beauty. His skin, although severely lined, was held with the most finely chiselled bone and the whites of his sparkling blue eyes glistened brighter than a child's. William followed the long white locks of hair draped over the man's most unusual clothes. They were tailored in the shape of a three-piece suit, its dark green hues in a material he had never seen. From the man's chest and cuffs, emerged pale leaf-like frills. William also observed a glow that appeared to emanate from his whole being.

'You!' said William.

'Yes me,' said the man, his voice resonating as if it had bounced from somewhere far away.

'Who are you?'

The man rolled his smiling eyes and mused. 'Someone, who has not been here in this sphere for a very long time.'

William watched, fascinated, as the man replaced the iron grid, seeming not to touch it and leaving it as though it had never been disturbed. William became aware of a feeling of time being lost, as if he were having quick black outs. One second the man was standing close to him, the next a few feet away.

'Come, let us talk.' The man moved to a nearby yew tree and resting against a gravestone that lay beneath its shade, looked casually about him. 'You like nature William?'

William was astonished. 'You know my name...how do you know my name?'

'There is much I know,' he replied. 'You have two of the carved wolves.'

William felt a little guarded. 'Why yes, I do.'

'Good,' replied the man. 'By tonight you will only have one.'

'What? I don't understand. Look, please tell me who you are and what you want from me?'

Again the man seemed to move unnoticeably and was now a short distance from him.

'Mankind has been robbing the Earth of its natural beauty, its resources, for centuries now. Within its finite form it thinks it is invincible, but it is not. No, William, Mankind might think that it's ready, but it has a way to go yet.' His hand rested on the edge of a tomb. 'A millennium has passed since wolves could support themselves upon this land. Those that survived thereafter did so fearfully, but not for long. The six carvings represent the last of England's wolves. They in turn, nature's breath - a breath that can travel through time. Their spiritual salvation shall be the beginning of hope for *yours*.'

'I don't quite understand,' said William, confused.

The man ran his hand along the top of the tomb.

'Their fate was sealed with a key, a key that can unlock great belief. For some this belief can be seen as inhibiting. Be aware, William, dark material forces abound at harvest time. You are not alone in your quest.'

'But what am I to do?'

'Trust yourself to find the six wolves William. You will be tested as the others have been.'

William's frown grew deeper. He loathed tests.

'What do you mean? What others?'

❀

'Trust yourself and be brave. You have already overcome certain obstacles and still held a conscience. Trust yourself and your feelings. All will come to pass.'

At that moment the latch of the church door clicked open. William turned to see the Reverend Rugby leaving from beneath the porch. William waved politely to him then quickly returned his attention to the mysterious man, but as before, he had gone.

Chapter 9

Betrayal

A tennis racket, a rather tatty looking play script, and several empty jam jars were all thrown from the passenger's seat of the Reverend Rugby's car into the rear, joining a shabby leather football and other necessary community wares.

'There we are William...park yourself there,' said the Reverend, as he wound down a squeaky window. William straightened the mottled seat cover before making himself comfortable.

'Are you sure you're not having to travel out of your way Reverend?'

'Oh, silly, of course not. I have to see the Reverend Gillespie. I went and left my shoes there again...Always do...Can't abide them, you know...Shoes.'

William's eyes dropped down discreetly to the driving pedals that were beneath the Reverend Rugby's feet. They were not only naked of shoe but sock as well.

'You see William, I always feel closer to the Earth barefoot.'

As the car pulled away from the church's side road, the naked feet dashed frantically between accelerator, brake, clutch, accelerator, brake... stall. The Reverend was not the most skilled of drivers and William could feel his own feet pushing nervously down on an imaginary brake as the Reverend drove unbelievably close to the vehicles in front. Had the Reverend left his glasses behind as well?

They eventually arrived at the farm drive and William insisted on being dropped at the bottom of the track to ensure that the Reverend would not be made aware of his now long absence. He happily obliged, waving, reversing and smiling all at the same time. William felt his heart, lonely in his throat. That would be the last smile he'd see this day, he thought. With head down he walked the track to the farm.

Outside the back door he could hear a concerned hub-hub of voices. He glanced at his watch - it now read three-fifteen. Feeling as if he was about to leap from the top board of a swimming pool, he took a last breath before opening the door to face the court inside.

William was met with a startled silence before a barrage of questions hurtled towards him. His mother, her face a mixture of relief and anger flew to him.

'Oh, William! Where have you been? We've all been worried sick!'

William peered at the questioning faces all anxiously awaiting a response. Flustered, he uttered the most obvious excuse.

'I'm so very sorry. I completely lost track of the time. I really did and when I got back to the car, you'd gone.'

'You lost two hours of time,' Leigh said. 'That's how long mum and I waited. Next you'll be telling us you were abducted by aliens.'

William hung his head in shame.

'You naughty, naughty boy!' declared Granny Phillips. 'I would have got a thick ear in my day...Come to think of it, I did!'

His father broke in.

'It's not been good William. We even had to inform the police.'

'The police!' echoed William.

His father gave a slow nod.

'Well, what with all these people going missing. Even during your absence we have received news of ...'

'Huntly Roach has gone missing,' interrupted Leigh, reaching for a biscuit from the tin on the table. 'His wife Sandy last saw him Sunday night before she went to bed. He vanished just like the others.'

Mrs Phillips studiously replaced the lid of the biscuit tin.

'You know, we really have been worried William,' she confirmed, pouring fresh tea. 'You have been behaving very mysteriously lately, staring into space and all that. Not to mention taking that wolf carving from Miss Pike's house.'

Alphonza, who had been sitting inconspicuously in the corner, started to nip and crease the hem of her skirt.

'Of course you shall have to return it,' continued his mother.

Having now caught Alphonza's eye, William could see she felt just as rotten as he did.

'We shall slip over after tea and put it back and talk no more of it.' Taking a pile of plates from the dresser she then turned to her husband. 'You had better call Constable Stone Bill and tell him the wanderer has returned. I'll lay the table.'

The scrape of crockery and the rustle of cutlery reassured William that life was about to return to its normal state, the trial being over. It could all have been a lot worse. That said, he was going to be losing one of wolves. But then, had he not been forewarned?

Later that day, holding the wolf pup in his hand and accompanied by his mother and the two girls, William set out on the short trek to Miss Pike's house. Mrs Phillips, noticing Alphonza's expression of regret, set about lifting her spirits by complementing her on how lovely she looked wearing the shiny pearl earrings that had caught her eye.

'Thank you,' replied Alphonza. 'They were a birthday present from my father. He did tell me they were for special occasions only.'

'And is today a special occasion?' she asked.

Alphonza shrugged her shoulders.

'No, not really. I just felt like wearing them today for some reason that's all.'

'It's William's birthday next Monday,' chirped Leigh. 'Granny is now thinking of getting *him* jewellery - collar chain and manacles.'

The damp forlorn odour of the house's interior highlighted the absence of life even more. Alphonza suddenly declared she wished to remain outside while Mrs Phillips, after stopping the door ajar to allow for air, followed her young upstairs to witness the replacement of the wolf.

Upon seeing it within its delicate tissue William suddenly had to fight off a dying urge to confess his experiences to his mother, but there in his mind was the wise smile of Mrs Gardner. The hatbox was put back in its rightful place and they abandoned the bedroom to join Alphonza waiting expectantly outside.

Mrs Phillips locked the front door and turned to the youngsters.

'Right, I think its home for some elderberry cordial, ice cream and Mozart. Yes, it's going to be my time tonight, after today's traumas,' she declared, heading purposefully back to the farm.

Much to Jackie Phillips' disappointment, a jumble of seven-inch vinyl records was strewn over the kitchen table. The anticipated calming tones of Mozart were superseded by the much harder, Stranglers, and Led Zeppelin. Bill Phillips was thoroughly enjoying himself wading through his labels of nostalgia.

'Tommy Andrews' cover band are going to be playing at the fete on Saturday,' he bellowed above the tinny throb. 'He's asked for suggestions for his rehearsal night tomorrow.'

Leigh started to enthusiastically line up her favourite records from her father's past while her mother searched desperately for the portable radio and C.D. player. Finding it beneath the table, she headed for the tranquil anonymity of the living room.

In order to be alone with his thoughts, William decided to take refuge in the confines of his bedroom, closing the door firmly behind him. William noticed that one of the dodo's had fallen from the bookshelf and broken its head clean off. Although easy to repair, it was a sure sign that the cleaning spectre had visited yet again. He tore a piece of paper from his sketchbook and finding a large, red felt pen decided on a ban.

"NO GRANNIES ALLOWED." Then in small print, "Those found trespassing shall receive a thick ear." In his imagination he could see his Granny defiantly tearing the sign down and he laughed out loud, his mirth being broken by a somewhat inhibited knock at the door. William quickly threw on a skeletal Grim Reaper mask and mimicked a deep threatening voice.

'Enter at your peril for the day of judgement is at hand!'

Through the holes in the mask he could clearly see a very sheepish Alphonza creep into the room, intimidated further by the surroundings. She closed the door. William, still wearing the mask, gestured for her to sit beside him on the bed.

'You don't mind me coming in, do you?' she asked, perching on the edge.

'Not at all,' reassured William, now in a normal voice.

Alphonza's eyes caught sight of one of the gargoyles peering questioningly down at her from the beams.

'William, I want to apologise for this afternoon. I'm so sorry that I broke my promise. I panicked. What with Miss Pike, Mrs Tench and now old Huntly Roach, I felt the wolf might have something to do with it. I was scared. Oh, William, please take off that mask, I can't see your face.'

Having forgotten himself, he quickly drew the mask away.

'Alphonza, I was scared when I took the wolf in the first place. That's why I made you make that promise. It's really me who should be apologising.'

'So who's forgiving who here?' They both snorted fits of nasal giggles.

'You know my granddad used to say that life's a steep road for sensitive souls, for they have to learn to live not only with others but themselves as well.'

Alphonza smiled. 'Well, I guess we've plenty to chew on, on this journey.' She then saw the picture of his granddad on the mantelpiece and was very startled to see a wolf pup beside it.

'William, you still have the carving! Why, I don't understand?'

He took the pup from the shelf.

'Alphonza, there are *six* of these carvings, or so I believe. This one belonged to Mrs Gardner, who happily gave it to me. That's all I can tell you for now because as yet I don't really understand any more.'

She stared at the carving, transfixed, her gaze interrupted only by the sudden movement of the bedroom door being thrown open.

'Why are you both up here?' exclaimed a surprised Leigh. 'Dad and me are having such fun with the records downstairs. Come on,' she ordered, before hurtling back down, William and Alphonza following behind.

'You know I really feel I ought to be going soon,' said Alphonza, as she passed the living room door from which could be heard the wonderful healing sound of Mozart. The house was soon propelled into shock with the thumping beat of a familiar rock track to which Leigh and her father were miming to joyfully.

Each to there own, thought William, as he headed for the garden to see Alphonza off, who, once outside, turned to face him.

'That steep hill that your grandfather spoke of William?' William looked at her with interest. 'Can you imagine?' she continued, 'Once you climb it the view must be truly amazing...super cool.'

'Yeah, super cool.' returned William.

Alphonza collected her bicycle from against the garden fence, next to which was sat an expectant Nellie. The day had nearly come to a close and very soon the curtain would fall on what had been quite a dramatic act.

Chapter 10

Insights

Even with much to think about, William awoke the next day from a heavy sleep. His morning priority, being a visit to Mrs Gardner's, soon drew him from his bed. He couldn't get ready fast enough and nearly fell over himself as he pulled on his socks, missing the Indian God, Shiva, by inches.

William breakfasted alone that morning for Leigh was still in bed having had quite a late night.

As he paced towards the back yard William could hear the hollow plastic thud of a football and could see Nellie watching in anticipation as Tommy Andrews, finding five minutes, was with great effort, kicking it up against the cowshed wall.

'Looking forward to the fete on Saturday, William?' he shouted.

'Absolutely, Tommy,' he replied, as he removed his bicycle from the shed, trying not to attract Nellie's attention who was barking wildly. But her sharp little ears heard the pull on the bike's chain, sending her frantic, as she now had to choose between a football and wheels. Football being out of season, she hurtled after the bike, making William pedal as rapidly as he could to avoid her snaps at the tyres.

Gently leaning his bicycle against Mrs Gardner's mossy wall he made to her door and rapped the brass acorn-shaped knocker. There was no response. He stepped back to see the window but only a mellow-looking Edward peered from within. Mrs Gardner has a life as well, he thought. He would have to be patient and wait for another opportunity to tell her his news.

Sitting astride his bike he drifted effortlessly down through the village. He could see the shop ahead and noticed a poster advertising the village fete. He drew up along side to see if there was any mention of Tommy Andrews' band, The Bicycle Pumps. He then heard the sound of the shop's bell and was hit with the hope that it might be Mrs Gardner, but the person who emerged was Sterling Price.

'Sterling. How are you? How's the wolf puppet doing?'

Sterling looked at him a little surprised.

'Oh, hello, Phillips. It's fine thank you.' He gathered his own bike leant against a small water receptacle that bore the head of a leafy-faced man, its mouth spewing water into a grotto-like chasm.

'Don't you think that man's face looks like the Reverend Rugby?' asked William.

Sterling pondered the water vessel.

'Yes, you're right, it does…same nose!'

The boys laughed at the idea as Sterling mounted his bike, kicking the pedals backward to fill the awkward silence that followed.

'What other puppets do you have?' asked William.

'Oh, quite a few,' replied Sterling, his unsteady eyes falling to his feet. 'They're not all mine though, and I'm not lying there. Mum had some when she was a child.' He folded his arms awkwardly. 'Would you like to see them?'

Slightly taken aback, William perked up.

'Yes, I'd really like to.'

Sterling clutched his handlebars and spun into the road. 'Let's go then!'

Within moments both boys were breezing down a hill, their shirts plumped out like sails.

Entering the tall gates to the Price's home, William remembered the incident on Monday. Smash's exploration of the house had gone unnoticed, thankfully, and reflecting on it purged any feelings of intimidation on entering the awesome building.

'Is your father at home?' enquired William, as Sterling ushered him through the front door.

'He's in London on business, which is just as well. You see, he doesn't like puppets.'

This time William had a better opportunity to admire the magnificence of the hall. His head fell back, open-mouthed as he peered up through its decorative gallery. He heard a door close from the landing above and looked up to see Chrystal Price appear from behind the banister. She was an attractive, serene woman, with a wave of rich blonde hair draped over one shoulder.

'Is that you Sterling?' she called.

Sterling immediately ran up the stairs to greet her, his hand dipping into his breast pocket to retrieve a small chocolate bar. They looked down on William standing amid the black and white tiles.

'Hello,' called Chrystal, her voice echoing. 'I don't believe we've met.'

A self-conscious William placed his hands in his pockets. 'No,' he coughed, clearing his throat. 'My name's William. I live up at Beech Tree farm.'

Chrystal smiled.

'Well, look after your guest Sterling.'

'Oh, yes, of course. Come on up William...I'll show you my room.'

Ascending the stairs he could see the occasional, very faint print of hoof marks, only noticeable if known but against the shock of the red carpet it did make him laugh a little.

Sterling's room was on the first floor. On entering it William was a little taken back by its blandness. The walls were off-white and bare and although the bed was an elegant period piece, its covers where made up of a plain navy coloured material, smoothed to remove all creases.

William watched as Sterling knelt excitedly down before a large metal chest that lay at the foot of the bed. Opening it, he pulled away several layers of clothing to reveal a box full of marionettes, on top of which lay the wolf. Aided by a chair and with William's help, they took some out and hung them over a heavy curtain rail. William was particularly taken with a skeleton and green-faced witch. He attempted to work her strings. Sterling was manipulating a Scotsman with incredible ease, making him drink from a bottle and wipe his chin with a silk hanky. He then hung the puppet along with the rest of them.

'You're lucky, William.'

'Me?' he laughed.

'Yes,' pondered Sterling, as he lifted a frog dressed in a red tailcoat from the box, 'you have your freedom. I've seen you and your sister about the village. You always look so careless, so happy just being who you are. I wish….' he paused.

'Wish what?' asked William. At that moment the door opened and Chrystal floated in bearing a tray of three tall glasses full of icy lemonade.

'The puppets…You have the Pelham Puppets out…Where's my little girl?'

Sterling reached down into the chest, brought out a frail ballerina and handed it to his mother. She placed it on the bed, positioning its arms and legs correctly.

'I was a ballerina once. That's how I met your father, at an after-show party. I thought he was so handsome, charming and wickedly dark. Yes, he quite took my breath away.'

She tilted her head as if lost in her past. William saw a deep sadness in her eyes, a sadness veiled by her pandered beauty and the affluence around her. She suddenly bounced out of herself,

'Come on William, tell us all about your farm.'

After having entertained them with many amusing stories and been given a respectful tour of the house, William was escorted by Sterling to the front gates where he noticed a hint of loneliness in the face of the village's new arrival.

'Come to the fete on Saturday Sterling,' enthused William. 'You and your mum. It would be great to see you both there.'

Sterling looked to the ground apprehensively.

'I don't know what my father has planned for us this weekend yet. We shall have to see.'

'All right,' said William, not wishing to be pushy. 'I'll say goodbye for now and once again, thanks for the puppet display.'

He kicked up his pedal and shot off towards the main road. After cruising a short distance he eventually arrived at the lower end of the village. Before him on the roadside he saw a figure alight from a bus and gather what looked like shopping, William recognised it instantly as Mrs Gardner.

'Hello,' said William standing from his seat. 'I take it that you've been shopping. Here, I'll carry the bags, you take the bike.'

'Many thanks comrade,' said Mrs Gardner bowing. 'There was a special offer on Edward-food. One has to gather supplies when one can.'

They meandered their way through the village, William telling Mrs Gardner about the cattle, the bees and his previous day's adventures. She listened avidly amid a staccato like chorus of jackdaws from the chimney pots above.

Edward was mewing wildly at the window.

'Tea William?' asked Mrs Gardner.

'Absolutely,' came the reply, and they both pottered through the doorway. Edward rushed to greet his beloved companion who swept him up in her arms and kissed his cheek.

'It's just not cupboard love with you is it, dear boy?' she said, as Edward pushed against her chin.

Mrs Gardner sat on her stool, riveted to William's accounts of the mysterious man.

'He said many things I didn't really understand, like Mankind thinks it's invincible, and that it's not ready yet, and has a way to go. What do you think he meant by that?'

Mrs Gardner took a deep pondering breath.

'It sounds as if he's talking about some kind of union, possibly a higher level of thought, a conscious level of wisdom between two energies. At the moment, one energy is moving faster than the other, creating an imbalance from which not everyone or anything can move happily forward...can grow.'

'I find what you are saying very hard to grasp,' said William. 'I don't fully understand.'

Mrs Garner poured tea.

'William, between you, me and the teabag, nobody does. Life's one big mystery. There will *always* be that which is greater than us.

Only the future can give us a better understanding and that's why we must play our part in the present to reach that understanding, that higher level. No matter how humble our role, we mustn't allow ourselves to be intimidated.' Edward jumped onto Mrs Gardner's lap. 'The tea leaves, lets do the tea leaves!'

'What are the tea leaves?' asked William curiously.

'Well, let's just say they used to advise me. Drink the remainder of your tea, William, and let's have a peep into what possibly lays ahead for you.'

Following her instructions, he then held out the cup excitedly for Mrs Gardner to read. She took a deep breath and turned the cup upside down, swivelling it this way and that. She then repositioned it upright sounding a 'chink' as it rested in the saucer. She peered in, muttering to herself.

'Ah,' she breathed pensively, 'the map reads like this: Yes, I can see the machinery getting very greedy, so to speak. I sense a man. You've heard of a wolf in sheep's clothing, well here it appears the other way around, a sheep in wolf's clothing. He has followers too, men and women, driven unknowingly by fear. Stand apart from them William, don't allow yourself to be drawn in. Your mind is your own…be brave.'

At this point she stared deeper into the cup, her face becoming quite startled. She looked up. William felt a shiver run down his spine.

'What is it Mrs Gardner?'

'Oh, it was nothing.'

'Yes, there was…you saw something…What?'

'Oh, William, dear boy,' she said, taking his hand. 'My imagination got the better of me, that's all. Please don't worry yourself. You know you ought to be going home soon…We don't want your mother worrying again, do we?'

'No, I guess not,' he replied despondently, rising from his chair.

Outside, William pulled up his socks and stuffed the bottoms of his trouser legs inside them, mounted his bike and stole a glance at the cottage. He could see Mrs Gardner smiling and waving from the living room window. She watched as he pushed himself off. Once he was gone, her expression turned to one of grave concern as she hugged Edward to her.

Chapter 11

Spying

The Egyptian Mummy that William was trying in vain to create looked rigid and tense. The newspaper body really needed to be papier-mâché and allowed to dry before the bandages were applied. Even the muslin he had discovered for that purpose looked too clean. Having found a good enough reason to abandon the project he scuffed it aside and sought something else to do.

Taking a book from the shelf he threw himself onto his bed and started to read but when he arrived at the bottom of the first page he couldn't recollect what he'd read. It was no use - he simply couldn't distract his mind from the whirlwind of questions within.

The sound of the phone on the landing was a great relief and he leapt from the bed to answer it but his father, a great phone-aholic, had reached it first, answering it downstairs.

William seized the opportunity. Pretending to be a spy he crept down the tricky stairs and drew himself up behind the dining room door. Through the slit between door and wall he could see his father chatting happily away. He then heard a suspicious creak from the floorboards upstairs. Bill Phillips placed his hand over the mouthpiece.

'Leigh, put that phone down now!' he bellowed. 'I heard you pick it up...That's rude!

Leigh replaced the receiver and stomped back to her room. After a series of acknowledging grunts, William sensed the conversation was coming to a close and started to carefully return to his room. After Bill had said his goodbyes, he made his way to the bottom of the stairs.

'Your uncle Rufus is coming down on Saturday,' he announced. 'No doubt he'll come to the fete in the afternoon.'

William and Leigh adored their Uncle Rufus, who, much to Bill's forgetfulness, loathed the 'Uncle' title. He was their mother's brother and a one-time heavy metal rocker. Tamed with age, he was still a rebel at heart, although mellow in his actions.

Leigh was ecstatic and leapt upon her bed to vent her excitement. William raced in and jumped upon the bed as well.

'Get off!' ordered Leigh, but William ignored her defiantly. Gathering one of her pillows, she struck him across the head.

'You monster!' he yelled, and quickly snatched the other for himself.

With lungs pumping and hearts racing they fought like crazed animals, that is, until their father, outraged, burst in.

'That's enough jumbo's…This house wasn't built for elephants. You can cut the circus behaviour out now.'

The youngsters fell across the bed panting, desperate for breath, while their father reminded them they would need all their energy for tomorrow. He and Tommy would be baling the field around Great Cheriton Wood and there would be much work on the farm. This news soon sobered their spirits. Any attempt for William to practice mummification would certainly have to now wait. Leaving his sister staring mindlessly at the ceiling, he trundled back to his dungeon and decided to make what time he had his own.

He pulled a large reference book from the shelf and having sifted through its sections, soon found that which revealed more about wolves. Adding to what he already knew, he learnt that wolves are great travellers. One animal was recorded as travelling one-hundred-and-twenty-five miles in a single day. He discovered that the leading wolf is called the alpha, the subordinate the beta, and that wolves have a strong community spirit, the whole pack helping in the rearing of the pups. From eight months the pups are taught how to hunt, the whole pack taking part. Finally, his study concluded with a picture of a Romanian wolf, reminding him of that fear-laden gulf, embellished through folklore, fairytale and questionable truth, that existed between humans and wolves.

The heat of late July was becoming more intense and that night was no exception. In a moment of shear restlessness, William flung his duvet cover off and sat up on his bed fully awake. The drop of a pin could be heard in the simmering heat. Sneaking downstairs would have to be carried out with utmost skill. Using the banister as a bridge over the river of creaky boards, he finally arrived within the safety of the living room and quietly closed the door behind him. Turning on the television, he nestled down before the screen. Before him the image materialised into a decadent lady vampire, drifting through the woods in search of her next victim. Just what the doctor ordered, thought William, as he watched the hungry creature hunt and discover a man through a forest of tall ferns. Finally clawing at his neck, she threw her head back to reveal a set of sharp pointed teeth. William drew his knees to his chest as the monster plunged her fangs into her prey.

With a shock William simultaneously yelped as an arm suddenly reached around his neck, hauling him to the ground.

'Grrrrrr!'

William turned to face his fright, only to see his sister in a fit of breathy giggles.

'You stupid…' he snapped. 'You could wake mum and dad…'

Leigh rolled her eyes casually and nestled herself on the floor beside her brother to watch the film. Feeling the room to be quite stuffy she ventured to open a window. Pushing it ajar, she looked out into the sweltering night. She could see the faint glow of insects hovering in the haze and glimpsed a bat dive into the darkness beyond. She then noticed what looked like a pair of large bright eyes flickering some distance away. She knew what they were.

'William, quick! There's a car just gone into Pike's drive!'

William jumped up to see. The house was now shrouded in darkness but then a light seemed to flicker from within.

'There's someone in Pike's house… Whoever could it be at this hour?' whispered Leigh. 'Perhaps the old witch has returned after all.'

'Maybe,' said William intrigued, 'I'm going to have a look.'

'I'm coming with you.'

'Oh, no you're not... It could be dangerous. Don't forget about....' William then remembered that Leigh new nothing of what lay in the pantry.

'I'm coming with you,' confirmed Leigh, purposefully louder.

'All right, all right,' replied William, giving in. 'But please be quiet.'

He watched his sister march from the room first. Soon they were outside and in the depths of the night.

Closing the field gate behind them, they paced across the grass, William wearing jeans, Leigh in an enormous white T-shirt that once belonged to her father.

'That's right,' he declared tensely. 'Let's make ourselves look really obvious.'

'Oh, shut up!' snapped Leigh, as she raced ahead.

Eventually they arrived at the hedge that separated them from Miss Pike's house. William pulled the barbed wire up high enough to allow Leigh to crawl under without tearing the outrageous t-shirt. They clambered through a hedge and positioned themselves behind a privet bush in order to spy inside. From here they had a good view of the house and could quite clearly see a figure move into the bedroom towards the wardrobe. The figure then vanished from sight, only to reappear moments later holding up the blue peacock dress.

'That's Livia Tench,' whispered Leigh. 'What's she doing in Pike's house?'

'I don't know,' said William. 'But she certainly has her eyes on those clothes.'

It was then that they noticed a suspicious shadow with a torch, moving past the window downstairs.

'Quick, get down Leigh or we shall be seen.' They both huddled on the ground, peering carefully from behind the bush to see who it might be, but the light vanished into the back pantry. 'We'll have a better angle if we move over to that closer bush,' exclaimed Leigh.

'No!' warned William. 'You'll be seen.' But she didn't listen and took her chance. There then came a sharp scream from within the bedroom.

Livia Tench had caught sight of the spectre-like white of Leigh's t-shirt. The lights upstairs were suddenly dashed out and the house fell into darkness.

'We have to get out of here and fast!' urged William.

Leigh doubled back to her brother and they both retraced their movements back to the fence. Leigh made it under but William found himself struggling beneath it, just as the figure from downstairs entered the back garden spotlighting the torch across the shrubs and bushes. William looked back to see the spotlight move in on them, the figure behind it still unrecognisable. The light flashed across their faces.

'Get down!' implored William. Leigh flattened herself on the grass, William beside her, nudged her in the ribs.

'Roll,' he whispered. 'Roll, roll, roll!'

They did, over and over and over the cool of the grass, until they arrived within the safety and blackness of the field. The torch's beam searched frantically for them but the two youngsters had now discovered the safe cover of Ruth, the tamest of the milking cows. Here they waited patiently for the threat of the light to relinquish, the eventual sound of car tyres screeching away signalling the all clear. They then made rapidly for home.

Having both successfully climbed the stairs, William closed the door of his bedroom gently, his sister peering questioningly by his side. William knew he had to cushion her excited look.

'For goodness sake don't breath a word of what you've seen tonight to anyone, especially mum...You know how she worries.'

'What about the police? There's definitely something going down at Pike's...Surely they should know?' whispered Leigh, as she observed her brother staring at the single wolf pup on the mantelpiece. 'I know you know more William, you can't pull the wool over my eyes and isn't that the pup from Pike's house?'

'No,' he insisted. 'Mrs Gardner gave me this, and I only know what I don't know.'

'What's that supposed to mean? I find it very strange that Pike has a carving the same as that one on the shelf and you tried to nick it. That's out of character for a start.'

'Keep your voice down. It's not that I don't want to share things with you, it's just that I don't know what I would be sharing.' He pulled back the cover of his duvet and slid into bed. Leigh immediately made to get in the other end.

'What are you doing,' he asked.

'Do you think I'm going to my room alone? We didn't see that film out...as far as I know, that lady vampire is still roaming the countryside...a countryside littered with wolves! Now budge your feet up.'

William huddled up begrudgingly as far as he could then reached up and turned out the bedside lamp while his sister stretched out like a cuckoo.

Chapter 12

A Gift from Nature

The two youngsters sat at the breakfast table very puffy-eyed indeed. Their mother had cleared the crockery a while ago and now threw a suspicious glance from the nearby utility room where she was busy loading the washing machine.

'I heard you muttering in the night you two. Well, we have a busy couple of days ahead I'm afraid. Your dad and Tommy have already left to go baling. He wondered if you could both clear the barn and milk the cows this afternoon.'

'Absolutely not!' teased Leigh as she searched for her favourite cereal. 'Getting children to work during their school holidays is pure exploitation... Bill Phillips should be jailed!'

'I second that motion,' said William, banging his spoon on the table. 'It's truly scandalous... I propose a strike!' The two youngsters stomped their utensils jovially in unison, while their mother passed through carrying the empty laundry basket.

'Cheeky mites!'

Outside in the farmyard they set about their allotted tasks, Leigh on an egg-collecting round whilst William headed towards the barn to start preparations for the new season's hay. He was just about to disappear behind a wall when he saw from the corner of his eye Leigh's bedroom window thrust open. He turned round sharply to see his mother's disgruntled face

'I'm going on strike,' she hailed, rolling out like a flag Leigh's giant T-shirt, the back of which was emblazoned with a green circular cowpat stain. Pretending ignorance, William shrank into the barn. After all, it was his sister's clothing.

Pulling away a few remaining old bales he found Mollie, one of the farm hens, with a clutch of newly hatched chicks. A sprightly little bird, she pecked William several times before allowing him to gather the tiny hatchlings. Leigh was on hand with a bucket to transport them to a safer home.

The splendid weather faltered not as the day passed on. With his mind occupied with work his thoughts of the wolves were brief, which was probably just as well, since he had no real clarity of direction. He wondered over lunch if the telephone would bear more news. Or perhaps a visitor would call and reveal some cryptic information that would push his journey on. In any case, something in his mind assured him this was the calm before the storm.

Leigh and William managed to milk the small herd of cows that afternoon with relative ease. The hum of the milking machine, with its timely pops of cushioned air, lulled one and all within the dairy. Only the beastly flies played havoc to spoil the working routine and the cow's tails had to flick frantically to disperse their torment.

With milking over, they both strolled back to the farmhouse and could see their father and Tommy Andrews arriving with the first trailers full of round bales. Leigh still found energy to flik-flak across the back lawn before they all poured into the kitchen for refreshment. Work would carry on until late that evening with Bill Phillips taking full advantage of the fine weather.

The day eventually came to a contented close and William lay on his bed staring at the blazing orange light behind his drawn curtains. The summer smell of cut grass, his mother had mowed the lawn, and the evening song of the swifts numbed his mind for a much needed rest.

Friday arrived with a pre-weekend urgency. Bill Phillips, having finished the morning milking session was now busy assembling the tractors and trailers. If he and Tommy worked hard enough they could gather all the remaining bales in before nightfall.

William had set himself the task of building a small, wire mesh run for Mollie and her troop of hatchlings. He walked across the dry back yard armed with tools, his keen eyes observing the tiny cyclones of dust and grass spinning delicately in the light wind. Aiming a tall stake into the grass, William drew a breath and raising his hammer, was suddenly struck by the ignorance of mankind and the loss of the wood. Encouraged further by his frustrations, he brought the thick metal head of the hammer down hard with a resounding blow.

The earth beneath received its first stab as the stake plunged into the surface of its skin. William, his mind focused, soldiered on, whilst from the safety of the small coup's wire mesh window behind him, Mollie watched curiously. He was about to deliver a blow to the sixth and final stake when he suddenly felt the presence of someone behind him. Startled, he turned and was astonished to see the face of Sterling Price.

'Oh, hello,' said William. 'How long have you been there?'

Sterling smiled. 'Not long. Your mum gave me the directions here.'

William dropped the hammer to the ground and reached for a nearby roll of wire mesh. 'Would you like to help?'

Sterling nodded happily as William rolled out the mesh, suggesting that Sterling grab the end. The boys circled the wire around the riveted stakes, securing it with staples. Finally attaching it to the body of the coup, the sanctuary was complete. William offered the string-pull of the coup's door to Sterling. Delighted to release Mollie and her young onto the prosperous grass, Sterling watched in wonder as like balls of cotton wool, the tiny chicks rolled through its forest. Satisfied with their labour, William suggested they return to the farmhouse for a cool glass of lemonade.

The sparkle of bubbles from the drink fizzed beneath the youngsters' noses making them feel refreshingly lightheaded. Leigh observed their new guest with great interest.

'Do you and your family like living in the village Sterling?' she probed.

Sterling pressed his hands between his knees.

'Yes, yes... I like it a lot...and I believe mum does as well. But I don't really know what dad thinks...he doesn't say.'

Intrigued, Leigh probed further.

'Why don't you ask him...then you'll know?'

'Leigh,' gasped Mrs Phillips, 'you really do take liberties sometimes.'

Noticing that their glasses were empty, William took the opportunity to invite Sterling to see his room and all three of them raced up stairs.

Sterling stood by the door of William's room, his eyes feasting with amazement. 'Wow! What an incredible collection... It's fantastic! Can I hold something?'

William nodded in approval and Sterling picked up a glossy model of a dolphin.

'I've never seen anything like this before.' He placed the dolphin against the figure of Charon, the boatman from Greek mythology who ferried the dead across the river of Styx.

'You have everything in this room,' observed Sterling. 'Light and dark, death and life... It's incredible!'

Leigh watched as he marvelled at the statues and monsters before him.

'Of course it's all junk,' she exclaimed to a rather startled Sterling. 'William makes them from rubbish...newspapers, loo rolls, wire mesh - junk.'

Sterling just couldn't believe it. He wandered further into the room to view more nooks and crannies teeming with creatures. William then remembered Sterling's puppets.

'Leigh, show Sterling your clown puppet. I'm sure he'd like to see it.' They all trumped noisily across the wooden floorboards to visit her room.

Leigh found the puppet in a sorry state at the bottom of a wicker basket. Sterling was more than happy to release it from its tangled turmoil. Leigh again bombarded Sterling with more questions, who gave only half-hearted replies as he relaxed in the comfort and wonder of her very different room, in which he felt quite at home.

'Tell me about your dad, Sterling,' pushed Leigh. 'Does he miss the city? Do *his* parents live there?'

Sterling stared momentarily at the clown's hand-painted face.

'They're dead,' he muttered.

Feeling awkward, Leigh and William said nothing and were quite relieved when Sterling continued, 'They were both killed when he was eighteen, killed in a boating accident off the coast of Corfu.' He made the clown's hand give a mock wave to William then pulled the string fastened to its back. The puppet bowed deeply.

The clock in the living room struck twelve. Travelling upstairs, the chimes reached the alarmed ears of Sterling.

'I really ought to go you know…mum might be worrying as to where I am.'

He returned to William's room for one last look. It was then that he noticed the wolf on the mantelpiece. Transfixed, he stared at it in silence.

'Are you all right?' asked William.

'Sorry, I just suddenly felt cold for some reason…it's nothing…I'm fine.'

But William sensed that things weren't fine, the wolf carving had worried Sterling. To ease his fear, he handed him the dolphin.

'I could see that this caught your eye…you can have it if you like.'

Sterling took the model and smiled gratefully.

'Thank you.'

Outside, small clouds had begun to gather, casting drifts of shade across the yard. Sterling mounted his bike whilst William clutched Nellie. Struggling frantically, she watched Sterling's wheels spin down the track homeward bound.

The afternoon once again drew to a close with Ruth being the last of the cows to pass through the dairy. William set about clearing any cowpats from the yard while Leigh grabbed the power hose to wash down the parlour. He then made towards the bulk tank area where the milk was stored and cooled. He assembled the various pipes in preparation for the internal wash. From behind him a spray of water propelled past the bulk tank followed by mischievous giggles.

'That's enough,' shouted William, as he pulled a bucket from beneath a sink and filled it with tap water. He then heard, with much relief, the power hose cut out only to be followed by excited screams.

'Quick William, quick! There's a huge grass snake in the dairy!'

Anxious to see their unusual visitor he rushed to look, only to discover his sister poised by the control of the power hose, which like a snake itself was coiled around her.

'Silly, silly, silly,' she sang as she flicked the ignition down. Her arm jacked back as a hard spray of water shot from the mouth of the hose, soaking William head to foot.

'You swine!' he bellowed furiously, as she screamed with laughter. William dashed into the bulk tank area and grabbed his bucket of water. Leigh's face dropped in horror as he marched back into the dairy with his bucket full of revenge.

'No, William, please no!' she begged.

'What you sow, you shall reap.'

Leigh ran screaming hysterically from the dairy pursued by William and the bucket of water.

'No, William, no please! These clothes are clean on today!' But it was too late. The icy cold water was flung from the bucket, hitting Leigh's arched back. She let out a wrenching scream as William, along with excited barks from Nellie, collapsed into a bundle of hysterics.

Their antics where soon interrupted by the arrival of tractors and wagons hauling more round bales into the yard.

'We're nearly done,' shouted Bill Phillips. 'I reckon a couple more loads should do it.'

Leigh ran back to the farmhouse hoping to avoid her mother, whilst William collected his bike and waited for his father to hitch up a new wagon. He then lifted it on board and scrambled up himself.

With arms held out across the wagon's rails, William allowed the warm summer air to bully his soaking clothes as his father travelled towards Cheriton village. They passed Granny Phillips who was out cleaning her windows. William called out to her but her mind was entranced with cleaning.

On they sailed, down past the church and manor towards the heart of the village. William could see Ivy Cottage ahead and was delighted to see Mrs Gardner outside pruning more roses. He waved to catch her eye and she immediately looked up and with a soulful smile, saluted.

The wagon tore on leaving the old school and the village shop in its wake until they arrived at the Half Moon pub where it bumped its way up the track towards the haymaking field. William jumped down to open gates for his dad and they passed through the field occupied by Smash and her gang before reaching a harvested yellow field that held the remaining bales.

Tommy Andrews was already busy loading a wagon, his frantic tractor-driving disturbing small parties of rooks, which from a distance looked like raisins upon the dry tufted grass.

Behind the working field lay the enormity of the great wood. William strode towards it. He hadn't visited the wood since last Sunday night and with Friday already into early evening he couldn't believe how quickly the week had gone. He then felt a sudden panic. Had he lost two valuable days in which nothing had happened? Should he have been out searching for another clue?

He arrived at the wood's perimeter fence and before pulling up the barbed wire, turned to face the cloud-filled sky. Feeling that the good weather was about to break, he sensed a turning of fortune.

Once inside the wood he walked beneath its leafy greenery, his eyes searching the uppermost branches for any trace of life, but all seemed still. The calm before the storm, he thought, but what kind of storm lay ahead? Did a storm mean a battle and if so, who would win?

He thought about the council meeting on Monday, only days away now. With a single signature, the fate of this wood and all the life it contained would be obliterated forever - obliterated by a civilisation that had taken more than its fair share and then slapped its Mother in the face. Running his fingers through his hair, William pulled on his locks thinking, thinking and thinking. What was he to do about it? What could he do?

'Who'll listen to me!' he shouted in anguish. 'I feel on my own here and who am I? I'm just a kid.' Tears broke from his eyes. Frustrated he reached down and unearthed a large dead branch buried beneath layers of old leaves. The strength of his anger held it up as he brandished it like an enormous sword, its weight slowing all movement. William, with all his might, swung it behind him then with all the energy he could muster drew it forward and like a questioning warrior screamed,

'I'm just a kid, a stupid bloody kid!'

He smashed the branch hard against a resilient trunk of a tree, where it broke with a resounding crack clean in two, sending the end half whirling, whirling and whirling extraordinarily high into the air. William watched as it reached its full height, where gravity took hold and it began to fall back towards Earth. Then, as if from nowhere, a glowing hand appeared, the branch resting in its magical catch. The moment was instant - William fell back astonished.

'My, we are angry!' smiled the now fully-formed mysterious man. 'Don't make hate your task master...see it for what it is. Then rise above it.'

William at first startled, drew his senses together.

'I feel confused, lost... I don't trust myself. I don't know if I'm right,' he confessed.

'Your time is right William... Is that not trust enough? You have the wise woman at Ivy Cottage to share your views. Allow me to give you another perspective.'

William then heard a rustle of leaves at his feet and looking down, saw a large grass snake coiling around a piece of wood. He stared, mystified, as the snake disentangled itself, slid away and disappeared into the undergrowth. William felt his body tremble as he bent down to pick up the stick. Carefully he removed the moss and dirt, he then truly shivered at the object before him, for there in his hands was the last of the wolf pups.

He heard the echoing voice of the mysterious man. 'Remember, if you take, you must then give.' William looked up to catch sight of the face of the mysterious man but strangely, as before, found himself alone.

Through the trees William could see the open space of the field beyond. Tommy and his father were loading the last remaining bales of hay onto a wagon. The sky above them was darkening by the passing minutes, looking like a black and blue bruise to the skin. A fork of lightening flickered in the distance and he clutched the pup to him. He would need to retrieve the others somehow and search for their parents. His quest was set but the sand timer had already started to run, each grain dropping into his heart. He would need all possibilities to reveal themselves before the last of the grains was to fall. William could see his father's arms waving to grab his attention.

'We've done here, we're going home.' Tommy and Bill had nearly finished their major summer task, whilst William was still in the depths of his own. Spots of rain began to freckle his face, so he ran for his bike to start the same journey.

With the pup on board, he sped down the field track to reach the village road. The spots of rain growing heavier, he hunched his shoulders and lifted himself from the bicycle seat to gain more pace, the road home being fairly steep.

'If I can make it home without having to get off this bike, then everything is going to be alright.'

The rise in the road past the church was a tricky stretch and he had to push on the pedals with all his might to climb it. Then there was a moments grace before the final ascent that led home. It had now started to pour, forcing him to shrink his eyes against the hard needle-like pelts of rain. His soaked trousers pulled against his legs, inhibiting speed. He stole a glance ahead to find where he was and could see the driveway to Miss Pike's house on his left. 'Nearly there kid.'

He was about to pass it when suddenly a pair of denim-clad arms reached out and grabbed him, dragging him into the cover of the drive and tossing him and his bike to the ground. William looked up to see the sly face of Troy Cruickshank bearing down upon him.

'Keen little bleeder, ain't you Phillips…snooping round the village like a proper Inspector Holmes… that's not to mention your little Miss Marple friend. Oh, I've been watching you I have… Yeah, right little keenie.'

William lifted himself from the ground.

'I've done nothing to you, Troy Cruickshank. You've no reason to treat me like this.' He started to reach for his bike but Cruickshank's hands snatched him around the collar, drawing William's face to his with furthering intimidation.

'Where are they Phillips?'

'Where's what?'

Cruickshank threw him to the ground. This time William landed on his bicycle, knocking the unfastened satchel at the back. The wolf pup fell out. Cruikshank's eyes caught it immediately. He bent down to grab it, but seeing his purpose, William snatched the pup and held it to himself.

'Give it to me!' spat Cruickshank.

'Never!' returned William.

Placing an arm around William's head, Cruickshank drew out his fist and punched him hard in the stomach. William fell to the ground exasperated, gasping for breath. The pup now was easy prey. Cruickshank plucked it up, leaving William doubled up on the ground in excruciating pain. Blurry eyed, he watched Cruikshank hold the carving up to his face.

'This one's a real beauty, yeah… Should fetch an even more beautiful price. You wouldn't believe the money I can get for these.'

He flicked a lock of drenched hair from his eye, smiled sarcastically at William then strode towards his dishevelled car. Feeling for the keys in his backside pocket, he turned and faced William pointing them at him.

'I know you, I know where you live and I know what you want!'

He unlocked the vehicle and slid inside. The car bounced as his body hit the seat. With a sharp grinding spin the car sped off.

Chapter 13

A Little Knowledge

Perceval, the farm rooster, was crowing wildly that Saturday morning. The first week of the holidays had passed.

William hadn't told his parents what had happened the evening before, instead he made quietly for the shelter of his room to dry off and recover from the mental and physical shock of Cruickshank's blow. Sleep had been patchy that night and unfortunately Perceval had found his way to the lawn beneath William's window and was creating another impending exhibition. William buried his head under his duvet but it was no good - his mind had been activated. He tossed his covers aside, threw himself towards the window and tore the curtains across to thoroughly scold the zealous cockerel. Joy beheld his sore eyes, for there beside the garden was Uncle Rufus's 1940's Norton motorbike and sidecar.

'Leigh,' he shouted. 'Rufus is here!'

A pitter-patter of bare feet on floorboards and the wiry sound of worn mattress springs filtered through the landing's open doors as the youngsters sat on the edge of their beds, eagerly pulling on their clothes.

The pair, now dressed, tumbled down the stairs together. Granny Phillips, half way up the stairs and armed with cleaning implements, had to throw herself against the wall.

'Strewth... If I'd known the monkeys had escaped I would have brought a twelve-boar gun...and good morning to you!'

Screams of 'good morning Granny' trailed past her as they rushed towards the kitchen.

Rufus Nelson, still in his leather jacket, sat in the corner of the dining area sipping a mug of coffee. Tall and lean, his long black spiky hair was only lightly speckled with grey. His piercing blue eyes lit up sending the skin around them, aged from smoking, into smiling crow's feet.

'Hey, wow! Good trouble has arrived at last,' he declared.

Leigh perched excitedly in the chair beside him, whilst William stood by the old Rae Burn, clutching its rail from behind, and swinging his happy belly out.

'News, news, news... I want to hear all your stories and what's been a happinin in the big metropolis of Cheriton?' said Rufus.

This was just the tonic William needed. Within moments the presence of their Uncle had bathed away all nervous thoughts of Troy Cruikshank. Soon the farmhouse kitchen was filled with hearty chatter, with Granny and Tommy dropping in for a swift beverage, Tommy reminding Bill that he'd be leaving soon to join his band for a final rehearsal before the fete and had anyone any possible final requests?

Granny Phillips, coffee mug in hand, stood up proudly.

'Yes, how about that lovely song by you know who.' Everyone waited with baited breath while Granny's face contorted madly. 'What's his name? You know... thingamajig... whatjamacall... whosehemeflop... You know... Doins!'

Tommy Andrews gulped back his coffee.

'That's all right Mrs Phillips. Actually, we already have enough numbers in the set.' He glanced at his watch. 'Well, I really should be off. I'll see you all later, then. Have fun.'

Granny looked nonplussed.

'Changing the subject,' she started airily, 'evidently Mrs Bramble's thinking of organising a village quiz. Yes, I shall look forward to taking part in that. Mrs Bramble has always admired my quick-witted general knowledge.' She gave a droll smile and ambled from the kitchen, her hand making for the duster beneath her belt like a cowboy reaching for his holstered gun.

Later that morning, Rufus and his two adoring fans retired to the garden to sit in the fine weather they were lucky enough to have that day. Rufus rolled himself a cigarette as William and Leigh poured their hands into a large plastic carrier bag, bulging with an assortment of books from the second-hand shop that Rufus ran in the city of Bath. Leigh occupied herself with a copy of Agatha

Christie's, Evil Under the Sun, whilst William flicked happily through the pages of Mary Shelly's, Frankenstein. As he did, he noticed a tightly folded piece of paper and plucked it curiously from its pressed shelter. Opening it, he realised he was holding a letter. He glanced across at Leigh, lost in the pages of her book, and Rufus, stretched out across the lawn puffing away on a rollie.

William read the letter.

Lavender House
Cheriton
June 18th

Dear Judith

    I do hope this letter finds you in good health and I apologise for having to write to you like this, however, I do not trust telephones and feel what I have to say to you should be written and direct. Firstly, I'm afraid I cannot help you with your interest in the location of your brother, as I explained my memories are unpleasant, I therefore chose at the time to rid myself of all knowledge of the event and sadly cannot offer you further assistance with regard to his whereabouts. However, I would like to draw your attention to a matter that causes me great unease. For weeks now I have not only felt concern for mine but your life as well. The strange and nasty calls I have been receiving from you know who, have intensified over the last few days, and it is with regret that I have to inform you that your name and the carving have been mentioned several times. Also, I only see it fair to warn you that your daughter Livia has formed an association with the troublesome young man in question, which can only lead to disaster.

    I am truly, deeply sorry that I have to write to you in this manner, I am aware that my reputation in the village is one that is not thought of kindly, but this bears no reflection on you and your discovery of me last year, I am not one to gossip and as a result your secrets are safe with me.

After reading this letter I do strongly advise you that you destroy it, for written words can travel far but they will always come home to roost.

What little love I have, I give to you and once again ask for your forgiveness.

Yours truly

Lucinda Pike

Your sorrowful Mother

William was shocked. Miss Pike actually had a daughter, and it was none other than Judith Tench, who, according to the letter, was looking for her brother. While carefully folding the letter, he shivered at the revelation. How strange that she and Miss Pike should be the first to go missing. William wondered who the troublesome young man could be. Could there be a connection with Huntly Roach? He felt desperate to share his thoughts but something told him to hold back. He would be seeing Mrs Gardner later, who always acted discreetly. He replaced the letter tactfully within the book.

'How did you come by these books Rufus?'

Rufus sat up taking one last puff.

'Some young woman brought them in. Bit of all right she was, in the looks department…frosty though.'

It must have been Livia, thought William, as he watched Rufus stub out his rollie in the lid of his tobacco tin.

'Are you all right?' Rufus enquired, as he lay back on the grass.

'Yes,' replied William, miles away. 'Tell me Rufus, what is your definition of fear?'

Rufus looked to the sky thoughtfully.

'Fear,' he mused. 'Fear, means different things to different people, but largely I'd say that fear is simply the unknown.'

William pondered his words.

'And what about greed?'

Rufus stuck a blade of grass between his lips. 'Greed? Well, greed I believe *is* fear. People are terrified of missing out and of being left behind. They fear what's here today won't be here tomorrow, so in that context, they take, take and take until the summit of greed is so high there's no going back. But there is a price to pay. Oh, flippin'eck William, you've got me off on one now.' He started to make himself another rollie. 'You see not everyone can, or wants to reach the material summit and these people have to find an alternative way of life. I just hope the alternative we discover is so beautiful that those up top will want to try it themselves and start to climb down from their material tower.' Rufus sat up and stretched out his arms. 'We've a long way to go yet but new beginnings are always worthwhile and we have to live in hope.'

William listened intently, absorbing what Rufus had to say. He thought about the word 'alternative', and wondered what lengths people might go to - negative or positive - to find those alternatives. Rufus had given young William much to think about.

Granny Phillips then appeared from the backdoor of the farmhouse, nose twitching. 'Come on you band of wild Indians. It's time for lunch.'

Chapter 14

Fate

The grandiose gates at the entrance to the manor house were shaded by the umbrella-like branches of the cedar trees above. The faint coo of doves could be heard amidst their canopies, lulling the air. The Reverend Gillespie, as if in harmony with his feathered friends, admitted the afternoon guests chirpily into the drive.

'No cows today then, Mrs Phillips?'

'No cows today, Reverend,' she smiled.

Granny was already busy purchasing a handful of raffle tickets. She sniffed the air expectantly.

'I feel lucky today, William,' she mused.

William didn't hear her as his attention was drawn to the beauty of the manor's gardens. The perfectly trimmed lawns gave birth to an abundant display of radiant flowerbeds, which at the height of their bloom upstaged the Georgian building itself.

He was enjoying the abundance of fragrances about him when a flurry of trumpet calls shot from around his legs. One of the manor's peacocks strutted through the thin train of visitors and took court at the lawn's edge. Throwing its head back to exert more shrills, the bird fanned its tail to reveal bewitching, shimmering eyes.

'Oh, showing off again are we Argus,' came an elderly dulcet voice.

Lady Lilly always knew how to make an entrance and gracing the stage from behind her feathered friend would certainly take some beating.

'Good afternoon, everyone. It's going to be a splendid day,' she trilled, her neatly coiffed pink hair jostling with each excited gesture. Seeing William she immediately waltzed over to him, her silk neck-scarf streaming behind.

'Oh, young William… How lovely to see you. Do come and see the stalls, as a would-be man of the world, I'm sure there's lots to take your fancy.' She then noticed that Bill was not present. 'Ah, your father not here today?'

William reassured her that he would be along after milking, at which she clapped her hands together and continued to greet the other guests.

Jars and pots and long thin bottles adorned the first of the many trestle tables perched upon the side lawns. The presentation of various homemade cooking dishes and utensils by the Patel's made William think of a wizard's apothecary. Mrs Patel a stunning woman swathed in a resplendent sari, spooned sauces onto pieces of bread. Having indulged in more than a sample or two, Jackie Phillips happily bought a few jars of the culinary treats. Mr Patel, a very handsome man, handed them to his daughter, who wrapped them and handed them shyly to a rather bedazzled William, who blushed profusely.

Leigh, Rufus and Granny entertained themselves before a table further ahead, which beheld corn dollies and other wheat-stemmed woven figures. Mrs Applegate, the round, ruddy-faced creator of these natural marvels, stood modestly behind her produce and almost gave a faint blush as Rufus held up one of her new and quite large boy dollies, suggesting that he'd probably done well in the fields. Granny had moved onto the adjoining table, which was in the process of being laid out with jars of fruit jam and glazed plaited bread.

'Just arrived, then, have you, Mrs Bramble?' she asked wickedly.

Mrs Bramble, a plump, breathy woman, pulled herself away from her hurried labour.

'The day be only so long Mrs Phillips,' she insisted, as she flicked a curious wasp from the shiny loaves. 'And for me it be never long enough, and that said, I seem to have mislaid my handbag *again*. Oh, darn it… It'll turn up.'

William could hear a 'ching ching ching' from behind him and turned to see Bob Gloster, the funny little moustached ice-cream man with a small red nose and potbelly. Adorned in ribbons and bells, he was traipsing off to perform a Morris dance. Nancy, his fat little Jack Russell waddling along in tow, looked really cheesed off.

William watched them skip heavily up some old ornate stone steps, his eyes resting at their zenith, where stood a pair of disintegrating classical statues. For a moment William allowed himself to dream that he was in the garden of Greek Gods.

'Their twins you know!'

William turned to see Lady Lilly standing gracefully at the lawns edge.

'Apollo and Artemis,' she trilled. 'They're twins!'

Curious, William swung round to marvel at the statues, only to feel his body shiver as the word 'twins' rang chillingly into his ears. As if in a trance, he gazed at their image, only to be surprised by the sight of Alphonza Pink, chest out, chin held high, springing from the cover of a shrubbery above.

'Oh, thou mighty God's of Olympus, the Earth presents its new creation, the Goddess Alphonza, Goddess of the chilled and hip.'

William immediately broke into laughter.

'No joking dudes,' smiled Alphonza. 'Lady Lilly told me I'm a dead-ringer for the lovely Goddess here.'

Plucking a piece of ivy and planting it into his hair, William dashed to the other statue.

'All hail,' he giggled, 'for I am the servant off the God Apollo, the god of prophecy and divination. There was a tiny kafuffle at the bottom.

'And I am the Goddess, Granny, allow me to pass.' Clutching her handbag Granny Phillips ambled her way up. 'Really William you are such a show-off sometimes. Goodness knows where you get it from.'

The upper lawns stretched out before a field fortified with more stalls and an assortment of various outdoor games, amongst them a pillow fight on a pole, coconut shy, and a maypole tangled with noisy children.

Before the backdrop of a large circular marquee tent, a number of people had begun to gather, William and his family joining them to watch a Morris dance. Here, ice-cream man, Bob Gloster looked a picture, his head bucking tensely with each step. Granny Phillips wondered why he bothered.

The afternoon rolled joyfully on and soon reached the hour of the children's annual costume parade; the theme this year being, Alien's from Outer Space.

Rosie Pink was on hand to help paint little eager glowing faces green and was met with one small disapproving boy who wanted his blue, a colour no one had at their immediate disposal. Mixing green, yellow and red together, Rosie, laughing wildly, quickly used her initiative and invented a colour that she insisted would eventually *turn* blue. The boy, not convinced, grabbed the paintbrush from Rosie and splashed the wet bristles across her nose.

'I apologise,' he said, studying her nose thoroughly. 'You're right, it is blue.'

Rosie looked astonished and watched, surprised as the little boy skipped happily off to join the other extraterrestrials. She then foraged discretely into her handbag for her powder compact and flashed her nose at its mirror - the colour was *not* blue.

William stole a glance at his watch. My how the time had passed, he thought. A little slice of fear told him to make the most of the day, as it wouldn't last. It was then that his attention was truly arrested, for Marcus Price and his family had arrived.

William ran to greet them but was somewhat frostily received, not just by Mr Price but Chrystal and Sterling as well. Feeling uncomfortable, he quickly made excuses to rejoin his family but before departing, William couldn't help but notice Marcus Price purchasing innumerable raffle tickets and encouraging a begrudging Sterling to do the same. William did think it strange but maybe they just wanted, like Granny, the privilege of winning the raffle.

Back at the games field, late afternoon was about to turn to early evening and William had returned just in time to watch the tug-of-war. The Reverend Rugby held up the centre of the rope while the men folk gathered either side. William was delighted to see the presence of Mrs Gardner, with whom he had much to share but for the moment she was busy recruiting more muscle for the tug-of-war. She disappeared into the marquee and soon appeared again with Tommy Andrews and the other Bicycle Pumps - Cunning Colin, Devilish Dave and Mischievous Mike trailing behind. Believing the two sides to be evenly proportioned Mrs Gardner threw up her arms to register the start.

'Just one second.' shouted car mechanic, Graham Parker. 'We've a man short this end.'

Bewildered, everyone rested their arms, only to hear a sharp reply at the opposite side from the butcher, Terry Ramsgate, who stood opposing the Reverend Rugby.

'Yeah, but you've got Samuel Applegate on yours,' he snapped.

Samuel Applegate took a size twelve shoe, was over six foot three and had a waist-size in excess of forty-two inches.

'Go on, William,' urged Granny. 'Grab on to the end of Rugby's team. I want to see these men work.'

William immediately ran to hold the end of the rope behind the size- twelve-shoed giant. Mrs Gardner started to administer the whistle but was interrupted.

'One moment,' pleaded the Reverend Rugby.

Everyone held their breath as the Reverend pulled up his gown and kicked his feet free of their sandals, prompting a mild wave of laughter from the crowd of villagers.

The whistle blew and the middle of the rope suddenly lifted. Shouts and screams filled the air as both teams heaved and pulled, Samuel Applegate's forearms flexing generously as the heavily-bound rope grew taught. The Reverend Rugby's naked feet dug defiantly into the ground.

'Come on men,' he wailed. A chorus of guttural, 'rhaaas' and 'heeeaves' were exerted from the creased faces as gentle hands gripped fast on the seemingly hot rope.

'We're nearly there,' shouted Terry Ramsgate, his team gathering more slack.

The Reverend Rugby's hands were being drawn towards Terry's. William pulled nervously behind Samuel Applegate. He could feel his tread loosening towards Terry Ramsgate's team, and he could see from the corner of his eye his subtly engaged Granny ushering him on.

'Come on, William! You can't lose! You've Applegate on your side! His rear alone is the weight of you!'

An outraged Samuel looked up and roared like a wild beast. William suddenly felt a slack in the rope, his eyes peaked forward and he could see Applegate's huge back looming towards him. The screams from the crowd thickened. The huge towering back started to draw nearer and nearer. William, sensing that the figure before him would, like a chopped tree, soon tumble, hoped to gain some distance and avoid being crushed. He trod his feet rapidly back on himself as, amid hysterical shrills, Samuel Applegate's titanic body began to collapse. The Reverend Rugby's team cheered triumphantly as they hauled their opposition to their knees to rapturous applause.

William lay some distance from the others within the comfort of the grass, chest pumping catching his breath. Eyes squinting, he looked into the sun and returned its smile, relishing a feel-good moment of life. Suddenly, he felt something drop by the right of his head.

The stench of nicotine pervaded his nostrils as a shadow drew over his face blocking the sun. Troy Cruickshank's denim-covered leg, stretched towards the butt of the cigarette, his thick-laced boot stamping it dead.

'Found some time to play have we Phillips? Shouldn't you be out there sniffing out those wolves? Forgot about the competition have we? Now that's not very wise…'

William leapt to his feet and Cruickshank drew closer.

'I'm watching you Phillips… I'm on your tail.' He noticed Mrs Gardner marching towards them. Flashing his eyes back at William, he made a gravelling sound, dropped a gob on William's shoe and then slunk off.

'Be on guard with that one,' warned Mrs Gardner, as she placed a hand on William's shoulder. 'Nothing but trouble can gravitate towards him.' Her eyes then widened, startled.

'All senses alert, William,' she announced, as she made her way towards something lying in the grass.

'What is it?' probed William, pacing after her.

'Look!' She came to a halt and pointed to an unidentifiable yellow object submerged in some greenery. They both peered down at it warily. Mrs Gardner kicked the grass prudently by its side while William knelt down to investigate further.

'Careful, William. It might be an incendiary device.'

'It's a handbag!'

'A handbag!' echoed Mrs Gardner.

Finding a dried teasel stem, William snapped it from its root and ran the stem through the straps of the custard yellow bag, lifting it from the cover of the grass.

'Why, my goodness… That's Mrs Bramble's handbag!' came a voice from behind. Lady Lilly's face looked aghast as she observed the bag.

'Between ourselves,' she whispered, 'with that dress she's wearing, it's a perfectly dreadful choice of colour. When it comes to style she really hasn't a clue, poor dear.'

'Look, there's a purse!' said William, retrieving it. 'It's open and empty!' he revealed.

'Ugh, gracious!' gasped Lady Lilly. 'You're not implying it's been stolen?'

Mrs Gardner raised an eyebrow. At that moment a loud drumbeat kicked up from inside the marquee behind them. Tommy Andrews and The Bicycle Pumps had started the first of their many sets.

'I think we ought to find Mrs Bramble, don't you?' concluded Mrs Gardner.

Back at the now retired trestle tables, a rather troubled Mrs Bramble did indeed identify the bag as her own.

'Oh, bless you. I know it be only a bag but am very fond it. Tis such a lovely colour,' she enthused to a discreetly smiling Lady Lilly.

'Are you sure there's nothing missing?' insisted Mrs Gardner.

'Nothing of any note. Just a few pennies…You see the majority of me tender be in the petty cash box here.' Her knee creaked as she bent to indicate the box.

'Of course there was the raffle tickets but then, apart from bingo, I never be lucky with gambling,' she chuckled.

With the mention of the raffle tickets, Lady Lilly's face shot a blank look. 'Ugh, heavens… It must be well after six. I promised the Reverend Gillespie I'd present the draw!'

'Well, let's get to it,' enthused Mrs Gardner, clicking her heels. 'William, I smell a rat…and I mean to catch its tail. To the marquee.'

An upbeat jazzy number filled the white tarpaulin enclosure receiving a gentle round of applause after its finish.

Tommy Andrews was about to strike up another number when the Reverend Gillespie graced the stage. Seeing this, Devilish Dave the drummer rapped out an entrée on his set which took the Reverend by nervous surprise and for some obscure reason he fell into a wee curtsy, which of course aroused a few titters from the gathering.

'Ladies and Gentleman,' he started, followed by a short cough. 'Many thanks for attending and supporting Cheriton's mid-summer fete. It's been a marvellous turn out and the many charities to which we subscribe to will be delighted with the collections made.'

As the Reverend continued with his speech, William noticed the Price family enter the marquee. Whilst Chrystal and Sterling's faces looked uncomfortable, Marcus Price's held a nervously alert expression.

'Right everyone,' continued the Reverend, 'without further ado, to present the draw, please welcome the much beloved, Lady Lilly.'

Devilish Dave again pinched the drums as Lady Lilly braced the stage to warm applause, followed adroitly by Mrs Gardner.

'Ah, it looks like we have Mrs Gardner as well, Ladies and Gentleman,' marvelled the Reverend, slipping his hands into his pockets. Informing him curtly that she was there to help distribute the prizes, she gave him a swift salute and put on her half-glasses.

After a brief speech from Lady Lilly, the Reverend Gillespie shook the box of raffle tickets while his wife, dressed in her usual full tweed suit, brought the third prize forth - a giant iced sponge cake.

'And the winner of Shirley Bakewell's spiffing sponge is...' The Reverend paused, as Lady Lilly delicately drew the first of the raffle tickets.

'Thirty-six,' she called. A short silence fell upon the crowd before a gruff voice shouted.

'Over here!' eyes turned to see Bob Gloucester plod towards the stage, little Nancy tightly behind, as Devilish Dave hit the drums.

Mrs Gardner dutifully helped Lady Lilly with the presentation of the sponge, while Mrs Gillespie foraged in a box for the second prize and pulled out, to her husband's evident disappointment, a very expensive bottle of sherry.

'You never really wanted it dear,' whispered Mrs Gillespie. Her husband's face looked most forlorn and with a reluctant tone in his voice he announced the second prize.

'And the winner of this splendid, marvellous very expensive bottle of sherry is....' Lady Lilly again dipped her hand into the box.

'Two-hundred-and-one,' a murmur of voices reverberated through the crowd, as everyone inspected their tickets.

'Two-hundred-and-one... That's me!' declared Granny Phillips, dryly.

With a large splash from Devilish Dave's drums she sauntered to the stage. The Reverend Gillespie smiled graciously, his cheeks flecking pink as the sherry was handed over. Granny Phillips peered at it oddly.

'And finally, Ladies and Gentleman, we come to the final prize.'

William's face lit up, Mrs Gardner's hand reached for her pearls, astonished, as Mrs Gillespie pulled proudly from the box a most extraordinarily beautiful carving. There were utterances of wonder from the crowd, for there before them was the mother wolf.

'And the winner of this rather remarkable carving, kindly donated by my wife, is…' The Reverend nodded at Lady Lilly to reveal the final ticket. William's heart was in his mouth as she held it up to read.

'The winning number is… two-hundred-and-two.' Mrs Gardner's eyes scanned the marquee as all the guests searched their tickets, Chrystal and Sterling Price obediently checking theirs.

'Struth, I don't believe it! Well, crikey…it's me again!' came an embarrassed Granny Phillips.

William felt like he was going to collapse with relief as his Granny stepped forward, accompanied again by a fanfare from Devilish Dave. On reaching the stage she suddenly swung round, and like a jubilant Queen, waved her subjects silent.

'I'm quite happy with the sherry,' she announced regally, 'let the ticket go!'

William's face shot white.

'No, Granny…take the wolf!' he pleaded nervously. Everyone gawped round to identify the raised voice, including Marcus Price. William felt sick with shame as all eyes fell upon him - he may as well have been standing there naked.

'Oh, William really…you have a carving just like that at home.' Marcus Price's eyes widened. 'What do you want another for? Think of the dust,' assured his Granny, as she rejoined her party.

'How very generous of you, Mrs Phillips,' hailed the Reverend Gillespie. 'Pray silence please while we re-draw the final prize.'

Once again Lady Lilly searched inside the box for the winning ticket. 'And it is…' Lady Lilly smiled.

'Two-hundred.'

Everybody roared with laughter, except William, who just couldn't believe the torture he was undergoing. All eyes fell upon Granny Phillips.

'Well, it's not mine,' she declared coolly. 'My numbers *start* with two hundred and one.'

There was a general hub-hub as everyone made final checks of their wallets, purses and handbags.

'Will the winner please step forth!' repeated the Reverend.

Then, from the rear of the marquee, a figure pushed forward. The Reverend's jaw dropped in silence and even Devilish Dave couldn't muster a grand finale drum roll.

Troy Cruickshank held out a tiny yellow ticket with the number two- hundred embossed on it. 'It's mine!' he husked.

The Reverend obligingly handed Troy Cruickshank his prize, whilst Mrs Gardner, like a squirrel, searched discreetly through the raffle books, only to discover that the yellow one was missing. A dull clap of hands came from the crowd as Cruickshank, clutching the wolf, motioned to leave. Marcus Price watched him with a deadpan stare as he left the marquee.

The drop in ambience was soon relieved when Tommy Andrews gave Devilish Dave a wink and the Bicycle Pumps began to pump out a distinctively upbeat, melodious tune. The dance floor was immediately taken up by the tiny green aliens from the afternoon parade. William, frustrated with his ill fate, manoeuvred his way despairingly through the excited, jumping galactic intruders, until he reached the safety of Mrs Gardner.

'Mrs Gardner, what are we to do?'

Calmly, deep in thought, she folded her half glasses. 'Hold fast dear boy, hold fast!' In truth, she hadn't a clue.

Chapter 15

Blue Moon

Having fully reaped the day's festivities, the guests were now feasting themselves on the various hot and cold offerings made readily available by members of the local community.

Samuel Applegate munched loudly on a slice of pizza and with a full mouth remarked, 'The whole worlds here, innit?'

Indeed it was, the Patel's were busy warming more rice to go with their notorious hot curry, while Mrs Bramble presented a selection of fillings from chilli to cheese to proffer her full, round, baked potatoes.

'You can't beat chips,' declared Leigh, as she tucked into her saucy supply.

'I can,' responded Rosie Pink woefully, as she forked her potato salad.

While everyone munched on their chosen fuel, the sky above mellowed to a deeper blue as if it too were preparing for the informal evening party.

The Bicycle Pumps struck up a cool smoochy number to start the evening dance and slowly people began to be drawn back into the cover of the marquee.

Having updated Mrs Gardner with all his recent experiences, a melancholic William sat on a sawn off tree stump. He would need to act fast now. Perhaps something as good as a miracle would come his way. Fat chance of that, he thought. He looked up to relieve his mind and could see that his father had at last arrived and was already in deep conversation with Lady Lilly and Mrs Gardner, all heartily sipping glasses of white wine.

He was about to pour himself a glass of lemonade when to his surprise, Marcus Price suddenly approached for polite conversation.

'Hello there…and how's the young would-be world leader doing? Interesting first prize, don't you think, William?'

'Yes,' he replied, feeling a little uneasy.

Price smiled, revealing his gleaming white teeth.

'So,' he probed, 'I gather from your grandmother you have some carvings just like it.'

William felt no reason to deny it.

'Yes, I do. I'm very fond of them.'

'I'm sure you are,' responded Price, momentarily sipping his wine. Then with a slight breath he asked, 'How many exactly do you have, William?'

William noticed his manicured fingers tighten round the bowl of his wine glass. He sensed caution.

'Well…' Before he could continue, Mrs Gillespie appeared gushingly.

'Oh, Marcus, you incredible beast. Fancy not telling us you were coming. And you've brought your family as well. You simply must introduce me to your wife.'

Marcus Price withheld his reluctance and charmingly complied. Mrs Gillespie made her excuses to William and trotted Price off to receive introductions. He watched as Chrystal offered her hand graciously whilst Mrs Gillespie, having suddenly lost the slide holding her hair, awkwardly tried to flick it back into some presentable shape. He then heard a trilling tone and saw Mr Price reach into his pocket to obtain a mobile phone. Leaving his small party, he sought a space free of ears to answer it. As in the Marquee, William again observed an intensity about Price's composure. Biting his lip, deep in thought, he turned to the drinks table for lemonade.

'Can you fill mine as well please?'

William looked round to see a rather sheepish Sterling beside him.

'I'm sorry I cold-shouldered you earlier, William. My father has been very tense all day,' he explained, glancing round to check that he was still on the phone.

William filled Sterling's glass and then his own.

'William,' began Sterling, allowing his eyes to fall to the ground, 'I hate my dad. I absolutely hate him.'

Shocked, William's mouth dropped open.

'I hate the way he bullies and patronises both mum and I. I hate the way he won't listen to what we have to say. He just refuses to share.' His cheeks flushed and eyelids flicked rapidly. 'I hate the way he's always right, too. There's only one point of view and that's his. I hate him William, I hate him!'

William was speechless.

Marcus Price's eyes caught his son in mid conversation. Replacing the mobile in his blazer pocket he quickly advanced towards them.

'Ah, good,' he prevailed, 'good to see you boys introducing yourselves. Did you know, Sterling, that William has a carving similar to the one in the raffle?'

Sterling remembering his unsolicited visit to the farm, shook his head nervously in denial.

'You know you boys really ought to get to know each other better…visit each others homes perhaps!' A silence followed, that you could sail a cruise ship through. It was, thankfully, relieved by Leigh and Alphonza.

'Not fancying a boogie then William?' teased Alphonza, stretching her arms behind her neck.

'Why not,' he replied, breaking from Marcus's side.

'C'mon Sterling,' insisted Leigh.

Marcus Price lowered his brow. 'You know this young lady here Sterling?'

Seeing Sterling blush red, Leigh quickly clocked the situation and lied.

'He beat me earlier on the coconut shy.'

Mr Price laughed sharply. 'Really! Sterling couldn't hit the potatoes on his plate let alone a coconut.' It was then that he first noticed a very self-conscious Chrystal talking with Rufus. 'Excuse me, I really ought to attend to my wife.' He stalked off and the youngsters immediately stole the chance to visit the now throbbing marquee, Sterling chasing behind.

Few people had shed their inhibitions to get up and dance - Alphonza was amongst the first to break the ice. Sterling held back, clutching his glass for comfort, whilst he watched the others make an exhibition of themselves. The first dance having abated, William felt a light tap on his shoulder.

'I'm still on the case, William,' bellowed Mrs Gardner above the noise of the band.

'That Cruickshank's after the wolves most definitely... Keep your eyes peeled and ears alert. I feel there's a lead here somewhere and I mean to sniff it out.' She floated gallantly across the dance floor with a glass of wine to join the Reverend Gillespie. The Marquee was beginning to fill with expectant faces. Any drinks had to be held tight to avoid being spilled.

William was again observing Marcus Price, whose strange familiarity had somehow seemed to intensify. The man was watching Chrystal, who had gone to replenish her glass at the bar.

All of a sudden a screeching wolf whistle shot through William's right ear. He turned to see wily Terry Ramsgate, beer in hand, staring goggle eyed at the latest visitor to the fete.

Livia Tench stood at the entrance to the marquee, her hourglass figure poised in a slinky black dress, her red bobbed hair worn up, leaving a lock to dangle suggestively either side of her face. All eyes looked round as she sauntered over to Marcus Price, whose forced half-smile dropped noticeably.

'Hello, Marcus,' she drawled, placing a cigarette between her lips. 'Got a light?'

Smelling alcohol on her breath, he scowled.

'You know I don't smoke.' He flashed his eyes over to the bar area and seeing Chrystal preoccupied unaware, grabbed Livia by the arm and swiftly escorted her outside.

'What the hell do you think you are doing here?' whispered Price, 'I thought I said...'

Livia's hand caressed his chest.

'I've come to be with you darling,' she said, her voice slurring. 'I'm tired of answer-phones and longed-for messages. I want you now. You're going to have to dump that pathetic Chrystal of yours soon, and I'm here to help give her the push.' She ran her hand round the back of his neck. 'I've done everything you've asked of me, given you all you wanted and I haven't breathed a dickie bird.' Her deep-red lips reached for his.

'No!' retorted Price, brushing her off. 'There's that one little issue where you failed to deliver the goods, proving that you're not to be trusted.

Livia's eyes winced. 'Oh, pook!' she spat, as she swung from the thick ropes fastening the marquee. 'I'm going for another drink. Maybe I'll introduce myself to Chrystal!'

Price went to grab her as she swung off but caught sight of a young amorous couple peering at them from behind a tree. He slunk back as Livia made to go inside.

'I hate fruit, don't you?' asked Rufus, as lumps of it fell into his glass from the punch decanter.'

Chrystal looked up, smiling. 'That's funny...so do I. Especially oranges... Far too sweet for me.'

'Savoury girl are you?' enquired Rufus, toying with the pieces in his glass.

'I do believe I am,' she mused, as she placed a lock of hair delicately behind her ear.

Granny Phillips was sitting by the stage, drink in hand, engaged in a very trim conversation with Mrs Bramble. The Bicycle Pumps hit out another loud beat, making her mutter in protest. Her quibbling was soon curtailed, however, by Samuel Applegate, clambering onto the stage to sing, spilling her drink in the process.

'Crikey,' she wailed. 'Oh, chivalry, where hath thou gone?'

Samuel blew her an exaggerated apologetic kiss and the men at the bar gave a rousing cheer.

'Really, some people have a cheek,' she snorted, before sharply eyeing Samuel's bum. 'And some people have really big ones!'

Bill and Jackie Phillips swung centre stage onto the dance floor, Bill nearly tripping over his own tipsy steps while Jackie fought to keep a dignified composure. The floor soon filled with couples as others leapt up to experience the jour de vive. Mrs Gardner danced with the Reverend Rugby whilst Lady Lilly made quick turns with the Reverend Gillespie. Mrs Gillespie who professed not to be a dancer, engaged herself with the task of concocting a less potent punch. A laughing Rosie Pink, who had brought most of the fruit, again offered her services as fruit chopper. She was indeed the culprit behind the much stuffed glasses.

Having retraced her steps inside, Livia Tench pushed her way through the bevy of happy dancers and headed towards the bar. She asked for a glass of wine, to which Graham Parker, standing in as barman, was happy to oblige. She caressed the glass to her lips as her eyes foraged through the crowd.

Removing himself from the hedonism of the evening, William stepped back to observe the action. Now inside, Marcus Price cruised along the inside edge of the marquee, watching Livia's every movement.

Livia, whose eyes had now seized Chrystal, lent her head to one side and began to stagger over.

William drew back to the rear of the marquee to take it all in. Price's dark eyes stared intently at the two women, and William, watching him, again felt a shiver of familiarity. His eyes then also switched to Livia and Chrystal.

Against the clamour of the band, Livia's words were inaudible. Chrystal's face held a mixture of bewilderment and concern. Marcus Price continued to stare at Livia. He then reached into his breast pocket and pulled something from it. William tried to determine what it was, but Price clasped his hands tightly around the object, pausing briefly before finally removing himself from the cover of the marquee. William made to follow him but was struck by a sudden mystified composure in Livia Tench's face. Her once contorted expression had become almost serene as her arms dropped to her side, her wine glass falling to the ground. Chrystal looked perplexed as Livia calmly turned and began to walk through the middle of the busy dance floor, exiting in the opposite direction of Price. Baffled, Chrystal shrugged her shoulders and turned her attention to Rufus who was rolling a cigarette at the bar.

William immediately searched for Mrs Gardner, who was still dancing happily with the Reverend Rugby. Not wanting to interrupt her, he withdrew mindfully outside to follow Livia.

The sun had now nearly melted beneath its flaming horizon and the early moon had appeared as if to wish it goodnight. Amid the few quiet revellers who had found solace in the gardens, William spun round in a circle, searching for Livia. He soon discovered her darkened figure standing alone and quite still, staring out towards the breeze-swept fields beyond. She turned her head gently as if determining direction, then, in moments, she was off, her body walking nimbly but strong.

William peered back at the luminous bustling Marqee. The Bicycle Pumps had struck up a rendition of 'Blue Moon', which echoed out ghostly across the village. Biting his lip, and maintaining a safe distance, he followed Livia. She plunged on without hesitation, effortlessly throwing open gates and travelling through acres of lush grass.

William found himself having to walk faster in order to keep up. On and on she ventured until she reached the recently cut grass that lay before the looming borders of Great Cheriton Wood, its darkened depths deterring her not.

Having made her way to its fringes, her fingers stroked the top of the barbed wire fence that prevented entrance, and she hypnotically felt her way down towards the mossy gate. Having released its chain with ease, she was soon beneath the woods leafy drapes. Arms hanging loose, she walked up the short track, which eventually dispersed into a thick of trees.

Following, but still keeping a discreet distance behind, William trod carefully on the dry brittle ground, for amid the cool leafy silence he was sure he could hear Livia muttering some kind of chant. He then detected another sound, that of a distant rumble, one that struck his body with fear - something was in the wood, something immense.

He paced fervently on, aware of something else - a pale shimmering light emanating from deep within the centre of the woods some way ahead. Livia was walking directly toward it.

A branch snapped heavily beneath his feet echoing loudly. He immediately withdrew behind the safety of a tree. Unperturbed, Livia moved on. William, not wanting to lose sight of her, left the cover of the tree, only to be jack-knifed back by its lower branches - his t-shirt had become fastened within its claws. He craned his neck to see Livia, but she was now barely visible. He slunk quickly to the ground and with a struggle relieved himself of the chastening t-shirt. Bare shouldered, he picked himself up and ran towards the now fading light. His desperate legs pushed on but what lay ahead now seemed to be dispersing. Even the grumbling ground appeared to be settling.

Breathless he eventually reached the clearing at the heart of the woods, but was met with nothing but silence. All that appeared before him was the imposing moonlit silhouette of his much-loved dead oak. Livia had gone.

Chapter 16

Rendezvous after Midnight

William could see the illuminated marquee, fringed with coloured bulbs, like some alien mother ship, a short distance ahead. Although his senses were still in shock, a sudden rush of wisdom grabbed his mind. As he approached, he caught sight of his sister cart-wheeling on the grass while his mother searched purposefully, trying to gather her tribe.

'There he is!' shouted Leigh, as she glimpsed him emerging from the darkness of the fields.

'Oh, William…where have you been? And where's your shirt?' grilled his mother.

He quickly assembled his thoughts and explained that he'd left it somewhere and couldn't remember where. She tutted and called for Bill, who once again was having a banter with Lady Lilly.

'Has everyone gone?' asked William.

'Yep,' replied his sister, performing a handstand against the now redundant maypole. 'The Pink's went ten minutes ago and Granny and Rufus have gone back to the car. Mum says they've both over-indulged.'

'And what about Mrs Gardner?' urged William. 'Is she still here?'

'Iya donta knowa,' implored Leigh, in a mock Italian accent.

William thought it better he returned to the car. Perhaps he should tell his parents what he just seen. After all, Livia Tench could be in serious trouble. He skipped down the Olympian stone steps, nearly bumping into a worse-for-ware Bob Gloster, who grunted like an old boar. Nancy, his little fat Jack Russell, now looked really peeved.

William crossed the lower manor lawn and was about to pass through the entrance gates when he was startled by the sound of crashing dustbins followed by the word 'blast!'

He slid behind a grotto-like water display, at the rear of which stood an alcove housing a beckoning sea nymph. He peered towards the manor house and could see a figure emerging from its shadows. It was Mrs Gardner.

'Oh, thank goodness!' he breathed.

Mrs Gardner stepped back startled. 'Is that you William?'

He gently assured her, safely guided her beside the cover of the grotto, and unburdened himself of his recent experience. She listened intently and then reassuringly held his hands.

'William, I've been on the case searching for that ticket book in the bins. I didn't find it but I did find this!'

She held up a newspaper entitled, 'The London Business Journal.'

'It's over a year old. I found it amongst a pile of papers of the same date. Lady Lilly is obviously having a clear out, but look!'

She held the paper towards the light of the moon to reveal a picture of none other than Marcus Price beneath the heading, 'Suspected Embezzler of Housing Trust Fund.' But Price's name was different. Pinpointed by Mrs Gardener's finger was the name Marcus Cavendish. William studied the name with interest, but not surprise. He had remembered Rosie Pink saying something about Sterling being upset over a change of name. Could it have been Cavendish to Price?

'Price has a suspicious history,' continued Mrs Gardner, 'and his immediate concerns for the future are, as you have observed, with the wolves.'

At that moment the voices of William's sister and parents could be heard as they trod the gravel drive.

'I've got to go,' he whispered. 'Mrs Gardner, would you be interested in my coming round later tonight?'

'Absolutely,' she responded, 'but only if it's safe.'

William scratched his forearm anxiously.

'Mrs Gardner, I don't believe we've any time to worry about safe.'

'In that case we'll buy some with luck.' She drew a coin from her handbag, perched it over her thumbnail and spun it high into the air. William watched it spin, its polished surface catching the moon's rich glow, before finally descending and plopping into the trickling waters below. 'See you later William.'

Having discovered her brother outside the churchyard happily puffing away beneath the old village stocks, Jackie Phillips drove her bevy of party animals up through the village's twisty road. Towards the climb at the church itself, the car began to struggle under its full load.

'Down with the gears, Jackie,' hollered Bill, as the vehicle chugged along.

She pinched her lips and grimaced - the last thing she wanted now was a driving lesson.

After leaving Granny and her fateful bottle of sherry at her much needed home, it was straight up to the farm. The car's headlights flashed into the quiet yard and a pair of wary eyes paced across its beams.

William opened his door and was met by a very stricken Nellie.

'There's something wrong with Nellie...she's shaking!'

Leigh heaved herself over the car seats and dashing to Nellie's aid, began to comfort the small dog. Rufus, meanwhile, had disembarked and taking some deep breaths and stretching his legs, was just putting his hands behind his head when he stopped in shock.

'I hate to be the bearer of bad tidings,' he said, 'especially after such a lovely day as well, but you've been broken into.'

Everyone gasped as they stared towards the living room window, which did indeed have a large jagged hole pierced through its centre.

'Now that's what I call a real sobering sight,' declared Bill. 'Come on...let's see what the swines have taken.'

Inside the living room Rufus kicked the offending stone that had perpetrated the glass. He then sat down on the sofa and rolled a cigarette while everyone scurried through the rest of the house to inspect various belongings. Minutes later they all assembled in the living room to relate the known damage and theft and were all surprised to conclude that nothing seemed to be missing. Much relieved, Jackie Phillips, fell back beside her brother on the sofa, while William perched lightly upon its arm recollecting to himself the strange incident with the bees at the Gillespie's.

Bill Phillips was standing in the middle of the room pondering possibilities. 'Maybe it was vandals, and nobody actually broke in.' He scratched his stubbly chin and yawned extravagantly.

'I think it's time we climbed the wooden hill,' he then said. 'We shall report it to the police in the morning. No point bothering them now. Right all…hop, skip and jump to bed.'

Within the seclusion of his room, William lay back on his bed feeling quite shaken by the events that had passed. He bit the inside of his lip, while his hand teased the mantelpiece by his side. He was then hit by a sudden thought and turning his head abruptly, realised that the one wolf he possessed had gone.

'Leigh, you haven't by any chance taken my wolf pup?'

Leigh was next door in the bathroom with a mouthful of toothpaste.

'Oh, yeah… I forgot to tell you, I dolled it up with lipstick and took it down to the Green Dragon and sold it off as a haggard 'My Little Pony… Stupid!'

William began to pace his room. The last thing he wanted was his parents to be involved. He scratched his head nervously then drew a clean dark shirt from his wardrobe. He closed his bedroom door, changed and sat patiently on the bed waiting for all his family to retire.

When the house eventually fell silent, he retrieved Miss Pike's letter from the book, turned off the light, threw open his window and peered out into the night air. Glancing at his watch, which had just turned midnight, he swung his legs through the open pane and made ready to jump, pushing himself hard so as to reach the vicinity of the lawn, only missing the thorny rose bushes by inches. Having 'shushed' Nellie, he made for his bike and spun quietly off.

He was so preoccupied with his thoughts that he didn't notice Rufus perched on his elbows leaning outside his bedroom window puffing on a final rollie, but he noticed William.

William thanked the stars when he saw that Mrs Gardner's living room the light was still on. Resting his bike, he gently rata-tat-tatted on her door. Edward immediately jumped to the window, as Mrs Gardner answered it hastily. Happy to see William, she motioned him inside and they both stood in the middle of the living room eagerly exchanging news, Edward observing curiously.

William handed Mrs Gardener the letter and broke the news that the pup had been stolen. Both of them suspected Cruikshank for sure.

Mrs Gardner pulled her half glasses from her top pocket, and sitting down, diligently studied the letter. After a few moments thought, she began her theory.

'I feel the wolves are all here, William.'

He seated himself down on the small stool and listened intently as she calmly continued.

'I believe that Lucinda Pike had two of the wolves and gave Judith Tench one, probably amongst other items as an acceptance gift, Judith having discovered Miss Pike to be her real mother. That wolf was to eventually fall into the hands of Judith's own daughter, Livia. And we know it now lies with Troy Cruickshank, an obvious contender for the wolves.

Meanwhile, we suspect that Marcus Price also has a keen interest in the carvings and you saw him gambling with Huntly Roach last Sunday, and I gather from your descriptions he won something very precious indeed and it wasn't plain old money. I know for a fact Huntly's wife, Sandy, was a collector of antiques. Arthur and I would sometimes see her at fairs, along with the Gillespie's. She once revealed to us that her husband often purloined antiques to pay off gambling debts.'

Edward jumped on Mrs Gardner's lap and she patted his head.

'So,' mused William, 'counting Livia Tench, that's four people suspected missing and counting the pup you gave me, possibly four known wolves.'

'Five,' deduced Mrs Gardner. 'Don't forget the she-wolf Mrs Gillespie herself had. Cruickshank has that now, and it was most likely him trying to burgle them last Tuesday. Somehow he knows of the wolves whereabouts. And he most likely stole the one from your home. I saw him hidden craftily away at the back. He was standing not far from your Granny. He must have overheard her mention the one that you had, then raced off to steal it, whilst you and your family were still at the fete. Marcus Price had an unusual interest in the raffle, he wasn't after any soft sponge or sherry. I truly believe, William, those two tykes are on the same trail as you.'

William bit his nails restlessly.

'But what about the sixth wolf?'

'That, dear boy, is a mystery. We know that Cruickshank doesn't have it because he threatened you while looking for it himself that Friday evening outside Miss Pike's. And we don't know for sure who was in her house with Livia Tench on the night you and your sister were spying. Livia, I suspect, had access through her mother. Anyway, whoever it was, may or may not have the wolf.

William stood up and looked out the widow. 'For all that Cruikshank's done, I'm not frightened of him...he's too obvious.' He then turned and faced Mrs Gardner. 'But Marcus Price does scare me.'

'He's certainly an unknown quantity. I feel we should investigate further, William, but first things first.' She re-placed her glasses in her breast pocket, then tore the letter resolutely in two.

'What are you doing, Mrs Gardner?'

'I'm honouring the lady's wishes.' She then reached for a match from the mantelpiece, lit the two segments and threw them into an empty grate.

'Poor Judith,' reflected Mrs Gardner. 'Not a bad sort at all. I wonder if she did make contact with the brother that the letter mentions.'

The Grandfather clock behind them chimed and struck one as they both stared at the flames, taking away the evidence of the ladies' pasts forever.

Mrs Gardner straightened herself up.

'Come on, William.' She then marched from the living room and into her tiny kitchen. William followed spiritedly. They both positioned themselves around a small table. An inquisitive William looked down upon its surface to where two black handsets lay, both connected to a recharging device plugged into the wall.

'What are they?'

'These,' announced Mrs Gardner, 'will be our only means of contact. They're walkie-talkies, a Christmas present from my brother two years ago.'

William smiled as he observed the strange gifts.

'Ask me no questions and I'll tell you no lies. My brother's a bit of a chip off me old block so to speak, or I his,' she laughed. She removed the now fully charged talkies from their rests. 'Right, William, gather yourself together. It's time to carry out essential investigations.' She handed him one of the vital communication links, flicked the switch down on hers and breathed into the mouthpiece. 'Testing, testing, over and out, comrade.'

William's receiver immediately lit up red as her voice echoed through. He then flicked down his own switch.

'Test received, comrade. Over and out.'

Mrs Gardner swung round and unlatched a small door behind her, the inside of which had an assembly of coats. She unhooked a long dark green smock and promptly attired herself, buttoning up the front.

'William, it's time for Operation Price.'

William's face shot with astonishment.

'Don't you worry, William, we won't push our luck.' She then returned to the open cupboard and disappeared inside, clanged about and then resurfaced holding what looked like a children's face-paint tray. She cracked the lid open and removed a hard dry sponge.

'Best camouflage ourselves. If anyone should find us scurrying over there, just say we're out bird watching.' She ran the sponge under a tap and mixed the colours blue, green and brown and dabbed their faces and hands lightly. 'Marcus Price is a man who sleeps little at night. When returning home with Lady Lilly from Mr and Mrs Cox's card-game nights next door, I've seen lights on and a figure moving around well past two in the morning. He's a lot on his mind tonight. Let's check his movements.'

They both filed vigilantly down the small hall and disgorged themselves from the cottage. Edward watched from the living room window as they braced the moonlit road, the dim of the night their only cover. William began to wonder where the mysterious man was now.

Chapter 17

A Face from The Past

During the daylight hours Marcus Price's house stood imposing but elegant, its angular design softened by the exposure of the sun. At night, however, the book bore a different cover. Its two high turrets either end spawned sinister tall shadows that seemed to lurch from behind corners and drop into cracks and crevices disappearing from sight.

William and Mrs Gardner stood before the intimidating black iron gates and peered through the railings. They could see a figure on the first floor move to the centre of a room and then drop completely out of sight, the light within following suit.

'That could be Chrystal retiring for the night,' said William.

'That's very likely,' replied Mrs Gardner. 'It looks like a master bedroom.'

Suddenly a side door was thrown open and Marcus Price stepped out. The two detectives fell rapidly behind one of the gate's immense pillars as Price looked out then crossed over to the garage, returning moments later carrying a bottle of wine.

'Sounds seem louder at night. We shall have to make a particular effort to be quiet,' remarked Mrs Gardner.

William agreed, as they stared at the awesome house. After a short while they noticed a light flicker on from the window of the right hand turret.

'That's the window where I always see a light,' said Mrs Gardner.

William stared at the window thoughtfully. 'I wonder if that's the 'get out room.'

'The 'get out room,'?' puzzled Mrs Gardner.

'Yes. Evidently there's a room that no one's allowed to enter.'

Mrs Gardner looked again at the house in wonder, while William searched for a possible entrance within the surrounding laurel hedge. He pushed through its exterior and behind the barricade of shiny leaves, found thick and spacious branches allowing space to crawl through.

'Over here, Mrs Gardner,' whispered William. 'We can get through.'

She followed his instructions and threw dignity to the wind. 'It's a tight squeeze but I can do it.' On hands and knees she forged her way through the undergrowth until she reached the open lawn beyond. Much relieved, she stood up to find her bearings and saw William waving her over to her immediate left.

'Keep as tight as you can against this far hedge,' he advised. 'We don't want to set off the security alarm.'

'Righty-ho,' she registered.

Huddled against it with a slight stoop, they tiptoed across, down past the side of the garage and through to the back lawns.

The garden at the rear was truly a sight to behold. Beech and willow trees stood majestically amid opulent shrubbery, the ends of their branches draping over a luxurious swimming pool, its cool sparkling water made iridescent from the spotlights below. Mrs Gardener quickly nestled herself amongst the shrubs for cover, William sidling beside her. From their vantage point they could quite safely see the house, its extravagant patio bearing open doors, fully lit from behind and casting light onto a round, decorative garden table upon which stood a corked bottle and half a glass of red wine.

'William, let's talk,' said Mrs Gardner. 'What we're doing is trespassing and I most certainly don't want to get you into trouble. I'm happy to turn back and consider other methods of investigation.'

'But I'm not,' replied William, as he pushed through the shrubbery, his figure now illuminated by the lapping pool. 'Going further is my decision, and it's a risk I'm willing to take.' He flicked the switch of his walkie-talkie and gave Mrs Gardner a salute. She returned the gesture. Like a cat, he then stepped lightly towards the house.

Heart pounding, he slid through the heavy glass doors. For a split second he thought of turning back but quickly arrested his fear and made his way through to the hall. He stretched his eyes up through the tall alcove ceiling. All the landing lights were off and he could just see a visible light coming from the uppermost floor. The 'get out room,' thought William.

He fastened the walkie-talkie to his belt and started to ascend the stairs diligently. Luckily the creaks were minimal, the sturdy carpet bracing his weight. He reached the first floor landing - all the doors were closed and silent. As if walking a tightrope, he crept his way towards the next set of stairs, which lay at the end of a hall. Reaching them he held the banister for balance and climbed.

The upper landing was narrower than the one below, which you could quite easily see if you peered over. William's eyes shot across to the far right end, where amid the darkness he could see a vertical shaft of light - the door of the 'get out room' was slightly ajar.

Should he go further? His nervous open mouth took a deep breath, which rendered him a little dizzy, and with the largest steps his legs could muster, he ventured on. He was soon nearing the lit shaft...only a couple more steps and he would be there...'creak'...William froze. The pores of his skin tingled with shock.

The vertical light darkened. There was movement beyond the door. Any sounds from within were lost by the heavy pumping thud of his heart in his ears. His dry mouth swallowed. The shadow beyond the door moved again, this time making distinguishable paper-rustling noises. He then heard, like a razors edge, the deep intimate voice of Marcus Price.

'Scalding please, I would like to speak to Mr Lambert Scalding.'

William, finding the audacity, took the final steps towards the door and peered through its vertical opening. The walls inside were a rich, deep red, like the colour of blood. He could see framed portraits of men, all of whom bore an uncanny resemblance to Price. Ancestors, perhaps, wondered William. The pictures circled a pentagram-shaped mirror, from which he could see the reflection of the back of Price's head. There was a slight swivelling movement, obviously made by a chair. Price started up again.

'Ah, Scalding.'

As preliminaries passed, William eased the walkie-talkie to a more advantageous position.

Outside Mrs Gardner listened with intensity, her only companion being the gentle lap of the pool. She turned the volume right up.

'Don't worry, Scalding…it's all under control. The contracts will be signed Monday, 6pm my time. The clause is worded accordingly. Don't worry…remember the Kensington scam…people can be bought you know…easily!' Price smiled. 'If we get a coin for every leaf from those felled trees, we're laughing.'

More formalities passed, then Price returned the receiver and relaxed back into his chair. William saw his arm reach out of view to obtain something. His eyes then widened in astonishment, for there in the mirror's reflection was the male wolf. Price teased its mouth with his finger. 'Nice little doggie…not long now and you'll be buried forever,' he sniggered.

William slid cautiously back from the vertical light as Price swivelled his chair round and stared deeply into the facing mirror. William peered thoughtfully at the reflection. The familiarity he'd felt so strongly about Price back at the fete again struck his mind. Then, a chilling shudder ran down his spine, for as if by some dark force of magic the mirror suddenly lit up. William flinched back. The moment was instant, but once the harsh light had subdued, the image of Price within the mirror seemed to emerge differently, revealing a reflection from another time, a face from centuries ago. William recoiled in horror. Price was the flaring eyed leading horseman from his dream, the very man who'd chased the wolves to their fateful grave. It was as if William had seen the true face of death. Price raised himself from his chair making to leave. Terrified, William turned sharply round and started to retrace his steps. He was about to descend the first set of stairs when he felt the light from 'the get out room' open out. Price was on the landing.

William shot down the stairs and speeded across the lower floor. Price turned the light of the 'get out room' off, and William could here creaky treads as the man strode across the upper landing. William was about to take the final twisting staircase when Price, alarmed, called out.

'Sterling…is that you?'

Heart thumping, William slunk back into the shadows as Price glanced hawk-like over the top banister. Unsatisfied, he started towards the next level. If William used the stairs below he would be seen. He had to think quickly. He plunged towards the lower banister and clambered over. Running his hands down the rails, his feet swung beneath and kicked the right hand pillar, his legs immediately groping round it for security.

Price was now on the lower landing. Sensing something he stormed across, pausing at his son's bedroom door. William's inconspicuous darkened hands clutched desperately at the railings. He felt Price's feet dangerously close. He heard the creak of carpeted wood - Price was about to descend the final stairs.

Frantic, William dropped his head down to glimpse the pillar. He released one hand and felt for a grip around its decorative pinnacle. Succeeding, he allowed himself to fall around its pole and drop to the floor with a light patter on the tiles. Disturbed, Price tore down the remaining stairs.

'Whose there?'

William shot along the ground floor and through to the living room, the open patio windows appearing like freedom. He slipped through and dived under the cover of the nearest shrubs. Price's presence soon loomed behind the tall glass doors and he hauled them wide open only to be startled by a black cat that sprang from behind a terracotta pot. Price hissed at its departure then stepped out onto the patio. He picked up the wine glass, flung the contents on the ground then retreated inside. In moments the lights of the pool and house flickered out. William was safe, for now.

Having relocated each other, William and Mrs Gardner carefully found their way through the laurel hedge and paced back through the village. Mrs Gardner's excited deductions were weighed with much concern as she listened to William's revelations.

'It's incredible... Price is definitely the very same man from my dream...and your suspicions were right Mrs Gardner, Price does indeed have the male wolf...and listening to what he said to this Mr Scalding, he feels confident that he can find the others. He still believes that I possess one and knows that Cruikshank has the mother. If he gets hold of that, he might find mine with it. That's supposing Cruickshank was the thief.'

Mrs Gardner didn't respond to his last remark. Instead she was lost in thought.

'It is...I feel,' she pondered, 'as the mysterious man explained to you...the image of Price is like the wolves themselves, travelling in time waiting for an opportunity or necessary point from which to release their energy. The pendulum swings left and right William but the hands on the clock face always move forward. In a material sense there's no going back. But human beings have the ability to consciously time travel. That is, to remember, reflect, to look back and learn. It's our awareness of the past that places us in the present, from which point we can prepare for the future, consciously.'

'I don't quite understand Mrs Gardner, it sounds all Greek to me.'

'You have to travel back further than the Greeks William. Their culture, like the Romans, was based on material gain, and egocentric like ours. It was the ancients well before them that had an intimacy with the land, an intimacy that heightened their senses. They treated the world as their friend. When we leave this life it is what we learn and give, not what we take that propels us forward. I heard Price on the talkie - the man's mercenary. He's after money and doesn't care who or what he destroys in the process. The man doesn't know it but he's caught in a self-made time trap. He refuses to welcome a higher level. There are many others like him, that's why there's an energy imbalance at the moment. Because of fear and greed, people are refusing to acknowledge it. Instead we continue to live in denial, to crush the source of all our lives, that being the planet...our home.

The paint on William's face began to contort and crack as he pondered Mrs Gardner's words.

'So what you're saying is that the two energies should be travelling in unison, as harmoniously as possible…'

'Or maybe as a whole. It's time for nature to have her say. We can't allow Price to obtain that key. He must be stopped!'

They made their way down Wisteria Lane, turned right at the end and headed towards Ivy Cottage. Mrs Gardner was feeling quite out of breath by the time they reached her front gate.

'Phew, it's been quite a night, William. I feel a little wheezy, not too good.' She lent breathy against the gate. 'Must be the pollen. It always affects me. That said, it was worth it, though. You've done well comrade…been very brave.'

William saw Mrs Gardner to her door. Edward was waiting for her return. She gathered him up in her arms.

'You seem a little anxious old boy. Never mind, I'm here now.'

William manoeuvred his bike into the road as Mrs Gardner turned to see him off.

'Well I think I need to make some notes on our discoveries, but I'll fix myself a nice little drink first and listen to act one of Bizet's *Pearl Fishers*, my personal favourite. It never fails to relax me. We'll speak anon William…goodnight.'

'Goodnight,' he replied, as he started to push his bike up the road, contemplating the results of their investigations. He stared questioningly into the timeless starlit sky. A warning then gripped him: Price was no ordinary man. He is supernatural, dangerously supernatural.

William reached the manor gates thinking that only yesterday it saw a hive of happy activity, but now everything seemed unnervingly still. He felt a sudden compulsion to turn inside the drive. He leaned his bike against one of the cedar trees and walked towards the water grotto, which he could hear trickling lightly. Peering over its side he could see the moon quivering on its surface. Beneath the ripples, Mrs Gardner's lucky coin gleamed amid the algae. William plunged his hand in to fish it out.

Mrs Gardner started to busily write her accounts of the last week's events. Word for word, she missed nothing and checked to see that every detail was thoroughly correct and secure.

William held up the tiny gleaming coin and stole a few moments to reflect. Then tossed it back into the translucent water. It was a memory he wished to leave, as Mrs Gardner had intended.

Chapter 18

The Shape in the Clouds

Having rendered himself bed-less, William spent the remainder of the night wrapped in sheets of tarpaulin, which lay gathered on one of the hay wagons beneath the covered yard, a very humble offering indeed.

He slept very little and was rudely awoken by small plops on his face discharged from a nest of swallow's directly above. Removing himself from his canvas cradle he glanced at his watch. It was 7.06am. His father was up - he could hear the hum and the pump of the milking machine.

He quickly made his way to the farmhouse and once inside the comfort of the kitchen, busied himself with the task of making a mug of tea whilst glancing out the window into the new dawn's tranquil light.

He thought about the wolves, the power of men and money. Power, is it so universal and who or what really has it? He wondered about the ultimate fate of the wood and the mysterious source of energy that lay deep within. A shiver made him reach for his tea, which had brewed far beyond his liking. He spooned the bag from the mug and placed it in a dish, which his mother reserved for such refuse. Apparently, tea leaves assisted the hydrangea shrubs to bloom beautifully.

Once inside his bedroom he closed his door quietly and made for the comfort of his bed, pulling the soft duvet around him. His heart was now fully with the wolves and the essence of their quest. He then fell into a short but deep shift of sleep.

Arriving at the breakfast table at a more decent hour, William was more than happy to share Rufus's full English breakfast.

'A great cure for over indulgence,' declared Rufus, as he tucked into his fried egg.

Bill Phillips, having finished the morning milking, entered the kitchen wearily. Jackie flashed him a sharp glance. 'And how's your head?' she asked, flipping an egg onto William's plate.

'Let's just say, I've seen better days!' he confessed.

Jackie Phillips laughed ponderously.

'You know one might feel envious seeing everyone merry and having a good time but to be able to sit down at the breakfast table the next day feeling as clear as crystal, is to have the *upper* hand.'

Rufus sipped his tea nonchalantly, wondering if Mrs Price had as sore a head as he.

Out in the garden away from the clutter of the kitchen, William perched on the stone steps to the lawn and contemplated his next plan of action. Sporting sunglasses, Rufus soon appeared from the house to join him.

'Did you sleep much last night?' he asked, shrewdly.

William, who was completely in his own world, broke from his train of thinking. 'Sorry, what was that Rufus?' he replied wide-eyed.

'Oh, nothing important.' He plucked some grass from the lawn and rolled it playfully between his finger and thumb. 'So, what are your plan's for today kido?'

William rested his chin on his knees. 'I'm not quite sure yet, I'll probably try and find some time to visit Mrs Gardner later, but if there's something you want to do?'

Rufus smiled. 'You're very fond of her aren't you?'

William nodded.

'Well if you can find the time, perhaps we could visit your beloved wood for a walk. Perhaps invite Mrs Gardner as well.'

At first William's face lit up with the idea, then second thoughts seized him. 'We'll ask Leigh and the others what they want to do first and then make plans.'

At that moment Leigh's bedroom window swung open and her cheeky face peeped out. 'I've no plans today,' she teased. 'Do you think Chrystal Price has any?'

Rufus flicked his glasses onto his forehead and pointed his finger jokingly. 'And you young lady don't miss a trick. You can just slip back into your potion boudoir and conjure up someone for yourself.'

She threw herself back into her room giggling heartily, her mirth only to be broken by the harsh alarm of the telephone. William looked up, startled. He sensed something wrong.

He could hear his mother's voice through the open window having answered it. Engaged in deep conversation, her tone was low. Between long pauses, William could hear the words, 'no, really,' 'oh dear' and 'I do hope so,' and after 'thank you for telling me,' the handset was replaced. Jackie Phillips then leant out the dining room window.

'That was Mrs Bramble. Apparently she saw an ambulance passing through the village early this morning. It appears Mrs Gardner has been taken quite ill.'

William could feel his stomach knot with worry as his mother's words echoed through his head. Confused, he sprang to his feet. 'Well, where is she?' he asked.

'The Avalon Hospital in town,' replied his mother.

'I've got to go and see her,' cried William. 'It's all my fault. I should never have got her involved.'

'Involved with what?' inquired Rufus, 'What are you talking about?'

'Please, I have to go… It's important that I know she's going to be all right.'

'William,' came his mother calmly. 'They might be only allowing immediate family.'

'But there's no one around here to see her. Her brother lives miles away up north. I've got to go.'

He ran anxiously into the house. Rufus watched, then planted his mug into some flowering aubrietia and looked at his sister. 'I'll get myself together and take him in the sidecar.'

Mrs Phillip's gave her brother a worried look.

'Don't fret,' teased Rufus, 'I'll remove the sunglasses.'

An anxious Jackie Phillips hovered over the motorbike's sidecar while William placed himself inside.

'Oh, do drive carefully Rufus. You know how I feel about that blessed bike.'

A helmeted Rufus nodded as his wrist twisted the accelerator and with his back arching forward they motored off, leaving a cloud of stones and dust in their wake. For William the journey in, although speedy, seemed to take longer than usual as every twist and turn in the road was registered heavily. He savoured none of the usual joys of the sidecar.

The motorbike braked with a slight jolt and settled neatly into a central parking space, its engine quietly purring. The white hospital building with its blue-sky backdrop seemed to imbue William with a temporary feeling of calm. He squeezed his head free of his helmet, noticing as he did Constable Stone leaving the building clutching a large brown envelope. Perusing through lots of hand written paperwork as he went, he looked confused, almost walking past his own vehicle. His chubby face quibbled as he realised his mistake. Whistling nervously as he climbed into his car, his heavy eyes failed to notice William and his uncle approaching the front entrance as he drove away. William took a trembling breath and entered the building. 'Mrs Gardner, please. I've come to see Mrs Dorothy Gardner.'

The rather mousy-looking lady on reception flicked through her register. 'Ah, yes…Mrs Gardner is in bay nine. Are you a relative?'

'No, but I know she has no immediate family living close by. I'm a friend of hers.'

'I'm sorry,' piped the woman, 'only family today.'

Feeling uneasy, William clutched his hand around his elbow then spun round to survey the bay numbers. Bay nine was immediately to his left. He frowned, then marched off in its direction.

'Excuse me,' squeaked the receptionist.

Rufus held out his arm to halt her calling security.

'Please, let's not make a fuss, I'll go and fetch him.'

As he paced down the corridor, William could smell that strange warm combination of surgical spirit, soap and school-like dinners, so typical of hospitals. He passed bay after bay until he reached number nine, a small area with four beds either side. Many of the occupants were elderly and asleep. William searched for Mrs Gardner and soon discovered her restive figure lying on a bed to the right. Her gentle eyes were closed. A nurse placed a crocheted blanket lightly over the bed. Upon seeing William the nurse's face lit up with a beaming smile.

'Oh, hello… You must be William.' Her voice had a sweet affectionate ring to it that could calm the most alarmed soul. 'Mrs Gardner has been asking for you. Grab yourself a chair and come and sit beside her for a moment. I'm sure she will come round for you.'

William found himself an easy chair and positioned it close to the bed while the nurse took an empty vase from the cabinet beside.

'See you in a mo… Oh, and by the way, Mrs Gardner was right, you do have amazing hazel eyes.' She beamed a bigger smile and left to receive Rufus who was standing in the corridor. Words were exchanged and they walked back to the reception area. William sat at the bed silent and motionless staring at Mrs Gardner's soft freckled hand.

'Hello, William,' whispered Mrs Gardner, her eyes opening slowly 'I'm glad you came… I knew you would.'

William felt uncomfortable looking at her directly. Instead he focused on the creases upon the bed. She touched his hand.

'It was an adventure last night. I've not had fun like that since I was a little girl. Thank you.' She breathed deeply. 'Listen William, the spirit of the wolves must be released. You will see the key, William, I know. Don't let Price beat you there and make a legacy of his own to further darken this Earth. Wherever Mankind is going, it can't go without Nature's honesty, her beauty.'

William looked bravely at her face.

'I don't want you to go,' he choked.

Mrs Gardner squeezed his hand.

'Try not to be frightened William. I'm really quite happy, but can I ask you to look after Edward for me, see that he's safe.'

William pressed her hand.

'You're going to be all right, Mrs Gardner. Edward is at home waiting to see you.'

He looked to the window at the end of the bay and was suddenly taken by the formation of clouds that had gathered outside.

'Look at the clouds outside, Mrs Gardner. There's a shape to them. Why, that one furthest away,' he leapt from his chair, 'looks like Edward sitting in the window. Look, can't you see the likeness?' He turned to see her response, her eyes were closed and she looked quite still. William moved to the bed hopefully.

'Mrs Gardner,' he whispered, holding her warm hand. 'Mrs Gardner.'

Mrs Gardner had gone.

Chapter 19

A Passage into Darkness

Rufus was sitting patiently in the hospital waiting room. He looked up to see the nurse ushering William in.

'Are you William's father,' she asked.

'No,' he responded.

'Oh, well, he's had a bit of a shock. Mrs Gardner has died.' She then rested her hand lightly upon William's shoulder. 'It was her heart I believe. Would you like a drink? Water, juice, a cup of tea? That's always good for shock?'

The mention of tea lifted his thoughts but they soon dropped again.

'No thank you,' he replied faintly.

Outside in the parking area spots of rain began to appear on the tarmac's surface.

'I'm really very sorry about your friend William. She must have been someone very special. People like that are very rare indeed,' consoled Rufus, as he handed William his crash helmet.

'I know it's not what you want to hear right now but it's good that you knew her.'

William peered up at Rufus, his face blank. They then both boarded the bike, Rufus flicking his helmet screen down with a sharp click. William felt numb. He just wanted to go home.

By the time they'd reached the farm the rain had grown quite heavy. Rufus drove his bike under the covered yard and with the aid of a large empty paper sack they both sheltered themselves from the downpour and ran for the farmhouse.

The day passed strangely on for William. Not wanting anything to eat he forewent lunch and sought the solitude of his room. Huddled up within the window seat, he watched the pouring rain. He thought about his granddad and the grief he felt then, but that didn't soften the blow. This was grief again and he had to see it through.

He gazed out of the window. It was as if time had stood still. He watched the swallows shoot out against the grey sky, snatching insects overcome by the deluge. The cycle of life continued.

The rain persisted into the early evening. Armed with a large black umbrella, William's mother drove him down into the village to collect Edward.

Mrs Gardner had once told him of the secret hiding place for the keys to her home and he had no problem remembering it. His mother watched beneath the shelter of the umbrella while William parted a cascade of dripping creepers to reveal the half-man, half-goat figure of Pan. He lifted the small statue from its base disturbing a long millipede and there, sure enough, were the spare keys.

Upon opening the door William was greeted by a rather desperate Edward. The silence of the house felt unfamiliar, almost otherworldly. The grandfather clock in the living room was still, the weights having travelled down as far as they could go, causing its time to cease.

After finding a plastic bag William, located Edward's supply of food and placed the tins inside the carrier and handed them to his mother who took them to the car.

He searched for Edward, who was perched on the stool in the living room, gathered him up in his arms and paused for a moment in the tiny room. Looking around he could see the parched remains of the letter in the grate and on a side table a small glass with the remnants of brandy distilled in its base. The quiet of the house soon overwhelmed him and he succumbed to a flood of tears. His mother had returned from the car and seeing his grief unburdened him of Edward, who looked disturbed and confused.

'He's lovely, isn't he?' she said to William, placing her hand gently under his forearm. 'Come on, son, let's go home.'

They left the house and William returned the key to its sacred place, carefully re-draping it with its forest of vines and creepers.

William felt it strange to have Edward back at the farm. It was as if he didn't belong. His eyes looked sad and his movements were uncomfortable and restless.

'Here, kitty kitty kitty,' sang Granny, as she tried to coax a reluctant Edward into sampling a saucer of 'Purdy Cats Best Rabbit.' Leigh was convinced Granny looked keener than the cat. It did look like the choicest pate, however.

The evening drew on and Rufus decided to stay for another night, much to Leigh's delight. The bookshop could wait until tomorrow. To occupy minds, a table was placed in the centre of the living room and Granny Phillips started to shuffle a deck of cards.

'Everyone agree to starting with a round of sevens?' she announced.

There were nods of heads and grunts of confirmation as Granny started to deal the playing cards. Rufus held the seven of diamonds, so he started first. In a short while all sevens were down and the rest of their sets were building up at appropriate ends of the number, but William's concentration was languishing. Even though he had the best hand, his thoughts being elsewhere made him lose many an opportunity. Granny had as usual taken the lead with only a few cards left to deal and William had to be nudged yet again by Leigh in order to take his play. The first game over William decided to retire to his room.

Opening a window to allow for air, he slunk across his bed, staring mindlessly into space. Occasionally his eyes wandered to his handmade menagerie, which seemed to peer back at him from various positions. Looking quite bewildered, the inquisitive gargoyles in particularly with their various expressions appeared not to let him rest.

He rolled over to stare at the blank wall. So much had happened within the last week and as his mind flashed images of all that had taken place. He sank further into a weight of despair, wishing and wishing the hands of the clock could turn back and with the present wisdom he'd gained, see that Mrs Gardner was made aware of not becoming too involved at her age, but there was no going back now, not in an actual sense. His grief grew heavier, weighing his head further into the pillow until, like the ashes of the letter in Mrs Gardner's grate, his mind had burned itself of any more thoughts.

The clock by his bed ticked on...ten, eleven, twelve, one, two... Then around three, William felt his mind stir. Restless he turned over towards the window and started to drift back into another passage of sleep.

That was until he heard something scuffle within the room. Alarmed, he opened his eyes but could see nothing, only the curtains gently rising and flapping in the breeze. A full moon shone beyond and he watched as they lifted once more and pushed a pile of papers from a stool onto the floor. This was the scuffle he'd heard, he thought, as he allowed his heavy lids to drop. He then heard a sound, a sound that sent a shiver down his spine - the distant howl of a wolf.

He tried to move to determine its direction. He heard a creak at the foot of his bed - something was definitely in the room. He lifted his head up to face the door. Nothing was there. Again the curtains lifted, cushioned with air. His eyes were then drawn slowly back to the door where a thin sphere of light began to form. William froze with fear, he stared as the light began to grow and take shape. He heard what seemed to be a near, yet far away voice echoing in his ear. Gradually he could distinguish his name being gently repeated.

William, William...don't be afraid.'

His head rose from his pillow until his eyes could better view the bright outline before him. William choked, astonished. There at the foot of his bed was the pale, glowing figure of Mrs Gardner. Tears began to roll down his face.

'No more tears, William. I've not come to see those. I'm here to reassure you that I'm still with you in spirit until it's truly time to go. Don't let the cloud of sorrow blind your path. The days grow short and shorter still. Darkness closes in and blinds our sight. Hold fast, William, in readiness for your next move... Looks what's behind you and you'll see further still.'

William reached out his hand, his eyes growing wide as the light at the foot of the bed faded away. He fell back onto his pillow and drifted into his final journey of sleep.

Chapter 20

Discovery

'**L**ook what's behind you and you'll see further still.' The words mulled over and over inside William's sleepy head until they reached a point that made him suddenly wake. His bedroom was daylight-bright. Without hesitation, he cast his duvet aside, raced to the window and threw back the curtains. Out in the backfields he could see a small tractor chugging along with a bouncy Nellie hovering around its wheels. His father was already busying himself with a new week's work. William pulled on his clothes and hurried from his room.

The landing was lit brightly from the wide open doors. Remembering his watch, he paced back to his room to collect it and was quite surprised to discover it was well after ten. He hurtled downstairs and made towards the kitchen hoping to find someone there but it was empty. He heard a distinctive 'meow,' and looked down to find Edward pushing playfully against his legs. He picked him up for a cuddle and instantly felt a small bruise in his heart. No, thought William 'hold fast.' He gently put Edward down, wondering what Nellie would make of their new companion.

He found a few pieces of bread in the breadbin and prepared himself marmalade on toast and coffee. At the breakfast table sat a large parcel. With all that had happened within the last twenty-four hours, he'd forgotten completely that today was his birthday. He wolfed down the toast and opened the parcel, careful not to tear the wrapping. He knew his mother was a great one for re-using it.

The young man's face gleamed with joy, for there before him lay an enormous book, the cover of which had a picture of a classical figure holding up a great atlas with the title, 'Our World and Our Universe.'

William was truly delighted with the gift. He turned the cover to find the inside embellished with signatures from all his family and friends and was quite taken aback when he discovered Mrs Gardner's name placed lovingly in one corner. He remembered the experience he'd had the night before, an experience that felt so real, almost tangible. He again recounted the words in his mind, but wasn't as yet in a state to acknowledge them.

William wandered thoughtfully into the garden trying to relax, knowing full well that today was the day that could possibly seal the fate of his ancient wood forever. He had until six o'clock to take action. He watched a solitary bumblebee, bumble its way around some tall flowering delphiniums. "Look what's behind you and you'll see further still." What did that mean? He turned to face the farmhouse.

That's all that's behind me, William thought to himself, the house and the kitchen, Edward, my bedroom, sleep, the spirit, my present... But of course, the past...the past holds the answers to the future...me needing to be in the *present* for it to transpire... into the future. What's in the past? Last week's in the past, amazing last week and this time last week I had two of the wolves. Now I've nothing but the present. But *from* the present I have my past to refer to. There's only one wolf unaccounted for, the one returned to Miss Pike's. I've got to start to retrace my steps somewhere. I must find the key for that house.

He dashed back to the kitchen. 'Now where could mum have hidden it?' He felt himself becoming quite agitated. He was trying too hard. He sat in his father's chair and relaxed, allowing his head to clear and inspiration to come to him. A parade of words passed through his mind... cupboard, tea, raspberries, kettle, rabbit, cat, Granny, cards ...cards! Diamonds, seven, King, Queen, Jack...*Jack*...Jack Phillips, Granddad, Granddad Jack. Excited, he leapt up from his chair and made towards the living room.

Placed neatly in a box on a bookshelf, William discovered the cards that were lying next to an old photograph of his granddad as a young man. William held up the picture and heard a light tapping-sound against its wooden back. 'The keys.' William was thrilled. He returned the photograph to the shelf and ran hastily from the house.

Running across the field to Miss Pike's house, William had to be particularly careful not to tread in any of the camouflaged cowpats that had nearly given away his sister's nocturnal pursuits some nights earlier. After some frog like leaps to avoid the hazardous spots he eventually arrived at the house's fence, and being so eager nearly tore his shirt stretching to get underneath.

Arriving at the front door he glanced wisely around before entering. All about the front garden seemed still, so he groped for the key deep in his pocket and placed its teeth within the lock. His hand was shaking and he had to push hard on the front door until it eventually gave way with a long creak. The smell of damp had now increased dramatically and the house seemed to possess a darkened gloom. Not wanting to hang about he made his way upstairs to Miss Pike's bedroom.

He could see that the hatboxes had been disturbed. Grabbing a chair, he began to forage around for the one containing the wolf pup. Finding it right at the back, he hauled it to the bed and gently removed the lid. As he'd suspected, the carving was missing. He was about to replace the lid when something sparkling caught his eye. Intrigued, he flicked back the layers of intrusive tissue and catching sight of a tiny object, he dipped his fingers in to retrieve it. Holding the object up in the room's dusty half-light, William felt his head swoon with the sudden realisation as to what he had between finger and thumb and to whom it belonged. For there, glowing as if fresh from the ocean itself, was one of Alphonza Pink's delicate pearl earrings.

He felt both confused and excited. He remembered that Alphonza was wearing the earring the very evening that he, his mother and Leigh had come to replace the carving. Alphonza had decided not to enter the house but to remain outside. He started to think of possibilities and questions that needed to be asked.

Carefully replacing everything as he had found it, William quickly made a final check of his footsteps before leaving the bedroom. Feeling a sense of eerie calm he paused momentarily on the dusty landing before pacing down the stairs.

On reaching the bottom, he had a strange sense that he was not alone and again felt compelled to pause for a moment in the dim light of the small hall. After affirming in his mind that there was nothing but the actual sound of nothingness about him, he took a nervous breath and holding the earring, decided it was safe to move on.

He'd only taken a step when a weird throaty cackling sound shot from a room some way beyond his right-hand side. William's body jolted with shock. He swung round so sharply that his finger and thumb pinched the earring, sending it flying high into the air. The earring hit the ceiling hard and then like a squash ball, ricocheted onto the stone tiled floor. The pearl snapped from its base and bounced onto the living room carpet. William chased after it but the pearl seemed to have a life of its own, racing on, bouncing over the carpet's string-frilled edge, heading out the back towards the pantry. William looked on, careful not to lose sight of it, and eventually found himself on hands and knees, cheek to the cold stone floor, peering between the legs of the sideboard, beneath which the pearl had vanished. Squinting, he could see the pearl's faint glow amid the thick cluster of a spider's web. His eyes focused further back into a small cave where William could see the beady eyes of the web's host. He stretched his hand underneath and carefully felt for the pearl. Feeling its form at the tips of his fingers, he plucked it safely free from the web hoping not to disturb its resident.

Suddenly from behind him came the harsh throaty cackle again. Frightened, William jumped right out of his skin as he turned to face whatever it was. To his shock he found himself staring at the raven. The great bird, perched stoically on the edge of the earthenware sink, stared at William. Not wanting to lose the pearl again, William fell awkwardly back upon himself, knocking the door of the fragile sideboard open in the process. A cascade of books, newspapers and private material spilled over him and onto the floor. William looked up sharply to see the raven squawk six times as it had done before, and then jump effortlessly through a small open pantry window, the light from which now cast itself freely over William.

For a second he paused in shock and then slowly drawing himself up from the floor, he caught sight of a gold embossed pentagram on the cover of a heavy, black, leather-bound book which had now slid from his belly, down between his legs and onto the floor. William shivered as he looked at the book's title - Magic, Method and Practice.

Chapter 21

A Question of Time

William stared cautiously at the strange, ominous book, shuddering at the words inscribed on its cover. Between the covers he noticed a piece of paper marking a certain page. Intrigued, he picked up the book and made for the ease of the living room to investigate.

Sitting himself on the piano's stool, he opened the book gently and was surprised to find a number of old colour photographs. To view them properly he held the first of them within a thin light issuing from the window. Although a little cracked and faded, he could see it was a picture of a young woman with raven black hair standing by the blooms of a pink rose bush. She was smiling joyfully in the sun, and was wearing the stunning peacock dress that Alphonza so loved. William felt his heart pinch with sad sentiment, for he identified it as being a young Miss Pike and she was, as he'd suspected, very beautiful - Lucinda Pike was once a very happy lady.

He shuffled the photographs to see the next and found another picture of Miss Pike in the peacock dress. In this one, however, she was not alone. Beside her was a well dressed handsome man, over whom she was lovingly casting her eye. William gave a tremble of surprise, for the man in the photograph was the exact image of Marcus Price, the only difference being that this man's hair was red and not dark like Marcus's. Shuffling through, he found another photograph of Miss Pike and the uncanny Marcus look-alike. It appeared they were at some kind of auction or fair. Trying to determine where they were, William carefully inspected the dressed tables in the background. It was then he really became alarmed - faintly visible on a table directly between them were the carved wolves. Again William responded with a shiver and anxiously shuffled through the remaining pictures to the final image, a photograph of newborn twins His mind reeled. Just what did it all mean?

As he held the photos an image of Mrs Gardner kneeling in her loft on the day of the very first wolf discovery, passed through his mind. He remembered her recounting her husbands words, 'He believed that every object held a story, just hold something in your hands and you will sense its history.'

William peered down at the remnants of the past and slowly a story began to take shape. He knew through the letter that Judith Tench was Miss Pike's real daughter and felt that one of the babies in the picture could be her. He returned to the photo of the newborns - one was a fair redhead, but the other had a mass of shocking dark hair.

As William remembered the letter, his face tingled with nervous revelation. Judith had a brother and the babies in the photo were non- identical twins, one a girl the other a boy. He looked back at the photo of Miss Pike and the red-haired man. Then things truly started to fall into place. Judith had red hair just like the man in the photo - the man was her father, and quite possibly the father of the little boy, that boy being, Marcus Price. William shivered, he suddenly felt alone and sorrowful as if something ghostly had inhabited his very being. But how had all this come to be? He looked up to gain insight, and then back down at the pages of the book. He flicked through and found an aged newspaper cutting placed neatly at the beginning of a chapter. He unfolded it and examined the headlines, which only startled him further.

Master of Black Magic Found Dead in Car Crash

William was even more taken aback when he looked at the picture of a man alongside the headline. It was the man in the photographs, Miss Pike's lover, and the name beneath was Flavian Price. William was right, the man was Marcus' father, but he recollected Sterling telling him that his father had lost his parents in a boating accident off the coast of Corfu. But of course, thought

William, Marcus and Judith had been adopted, the people who were killed, or even worse perhaps, murdered in the boating accident, must have been his adoptive parents, and their name was Cavendish. Mrs Gardner had confirmed this with the discovery of the newspaper. Marcus, like Judith, had found his real parentage, so he decided to reclaim his real father's surname, Price. He did this conveniently after his London embezzlement scams.

William felt compelled to read the article. Browsing through the print, he learnt that Flavian Price was the head of a secret magic circle and that he fatal car crash was over forty years ago, perhaps, thought William, before the twins were born.

He discovered that there was no known reason for the crash. Neither drink nor bad weather was cited. William looked again at the newspaper picture. Flavian Price had a handsome but cold face, just like his son. No doubt he'd jilted Lucinda Pike after discovering her pregnant with the twins.

William replaced the paper cutting studiously back into the book and noticed the title of the chapter where it had been placed, 'Protection Through The Waxen Image.' Studying the title, everything suddenly became clear to William. Miss Pike was using witchcraft to protect herself from Marcus Price, her own son. He remembered Mrs Gardner believing that Price, through greed, was trapped in some kind of time warp. Flavian and Marcus may as well have been the same man, the same negative greedy spirit. From what he saw at the Price's house that night, Marcus has inherited his father's ability to use magic negatively for his own ends. For some reason he desperately needed the wolves to further his power. The owner of the full set of six carvings was once Lucinda Pike. Perhaps it was her that had purchased them at the auction and this was where she had first met Flavian. To get his hands on the carvings, he'd embarked on a passionate romance with her. After revealing to Flavian that she was pregnant with the twins, she may have detected his true greedy intentions. So hurt, she may even have initiated the car crash.

Strangely, years after his death, she decided to divide the six carvings, distributing them at various auctions and antique fairs in the area. That's how Arthur Gardner, Sandy Roach and Mrs Gillespie came by them. But what about Cruickshank? He, along with me, knows their worth, thought William. Price has contenders.

Wary of the time William leapt abruptly from the stool and replaced the books and newspapers from where they had fallen. He closed the pantry window and ran back into the living room to locate the earring's base. Having found it, he quietly locked the front door and made decisively toward home.

His nerves made him feel a little giddy. He'd unearthed a piece of history that was very dangerous indeed and he truly wondered about the lives of all the people who'd gone missing.

On his return to the farmhouse, William found his mother and sister busy in the kitchen unloading groceries from bags strewn across the table.

'Here's the birthday boy,' sang Leigh, holding up a plump loaf as William appeared from the garden.

'Oh, happy birthday,' congratulated his mother. 'You were in such a deep sleep this morning we felt it best not to disturb you.'

'Thank you for that - I really needed the rest. And thank you for the fantastic present. It's just what I wanted,' enthused William, as he quickly helped them unpack the remainder of the shopping.

Removing a large packet of cereal from the corner chair, his sister noticed a set of keys perched vulnerably on the side of the seat.

'Whose keys are these left for the world to take,' she hailed.

William, whose mind was full, felt a sudden panic as he watched his mother gather what could be evidence against him.

'Oh, silly Rufus. These are his keys for the shop,' revealed his mother. 'He's left them before. Thank goodness he doesn't wear a wig - he'd leave that too.'

William felt deep into his trouser pocket, and was much relieved to find at the tip of his fingers Miss Pike's keys. 'Just slipping up to my room,' he announced, as he prudently left the kitchen to replace the keys behind his granddad's picture.

Having covered that task, William now wished to follow up the reason for discovering the earring. He ran upstairs to use the more private telephone on the landing. He found Alphonza's mobile number in his sister's fox-faced address book and dialled it anxiously. It rang and rang. Fearing no answer, William had to calm himself and was about to give up when he then heard a reply.

'Hello!'

William kept his voice low. 'Alphonza? It's me...William.'

'Oh, William... Happy birthday. But it's not, is it? I heard about Mrs Gardner. I'm so very sorry.'

He paused for a moment, 'Alphonza, I must see you today.'

'But of course. I want to give you your present, which is my way of saying sorry.'

'What do you mean?'

'I have something you wanted, William, and I feel I know how important it is to you.'

He was startled by her words. 'Can I come round now?'

'No problem.'

'Good... I'll see you in, let's say, about twenty minutes.'

'See you then.'

Before he replaced the receiver he thought he heard a click on the line. 'Leigh is that you?' he called out, but there was no response. He collected his thoughts and immediately rushed back downstairs to the kitchen.

'I'm going out for a while,' said William to his mother, as he pulled his socks over trousers. 'Hopefully, I won't be too long.'

Leigh, who was browsing through William's marvellous new encyclopaedia, perked up as he was about to race out the door.

'Where are you going?' she probed, as the phone in the dining room started to ring.

'Oh, the woods... I'm going to the woods,' he replied, stumbling backwards and nearly falling over himself. She threw him a suspicious glance as she watched him disappear beyond the garden. Mrs Phillips meanwhile went to answer the insistent phone while a curious Leigh stopped in her thoughts when she heard her mother's voice drop to a rather serious tone.

'Really…right…yes…yes…yes…no, of course I understand completely, I'll do exactly as you ask. Thank you for warning me, Constable Stone. Bye.' She replaced the receiver and turned to an inquisitive Leigh. 'That was Constable Stone.'

'Constable Stone you say,' replied Leigh, acting as if she hadn't overheard.

'Yes,' declared her mother as she marched purposefully back up into the kitchen and out into the garden. 'Under no circumstances is William to leave the house.'

But having more than efficiently escaped Nellie, the birthday boy had gone and was well on his way, speeding as fast as he could down the main road. He travelled so fast that even the insects floating casually in the air couldn't move swiftly enough out of his way and he felt the occasional buzzing wing scuff past his face. Having sailed beyond the vicarage he was just about to approach the Price's house when suddenly a yellow mini cab pulled hazardously out from the Court House drive. Alarmed, William squeezed on his brakes. The bike screeched to a halt, very nearly plunging him over the handlebars. He stopped only inches from the mini cab.

'Good God!' cried a horrified Chrystal, sitting next to Sterling in the rear of the cab. 'You could have been killed!'

'Whatever's the matter?' asked a concerned Sterling. 'You look like you're on some serious mission.'

'Sorry,' responded a breathless William. 'I guess I must have underestimated my speed.'

William noticed they were both wearing bright holiday clothes. 'Are you going away or something?' he asked.

'Yes,' beamed Sterling. 'We're going abroad for a week. But best of all, dad won't be joining us until the very last two days. He has business.' His smile grew wider. 'Oh, and happy birthday, by the way.'

'How did you know?' enquired William.

'Rosie…she's inside cleaning,' said Sterling.

William looked up at the house where through one of the windows he could see Rosie Pink, feather duster in hand, laughing away.

Chrystal leant over her son and said apologetically, 'We really should be off William, otherwise we'll miss the plane. Do give your uncle Rufus my love when you see him next.' A slight twinkle lit her eyes as the car started to pull out of the Court House drive.

'Where are you going on holiday?' shouted William.

Sterling wound his window down as far as it would go and leaned out, his hair tussling in the wind. 'Corfu,' he shouted, as the car sped off into the distance.

William felt the blood drain from his face. There really was no time to waste now. He had to get to Alphonza, and quick. Peddling nervously on down the road, he desperately tried to control his emotions as thoughts of hopelessness filled his mind like the rise of drowning water in a tank.

He was nearing the major crossroads that only a week before could have witnessed a catastrophic collision of cattle. Here, one week on, he had a different drama to deal with. Bob Glosters ice-cream van was travelling ahead and William found himself cycling right up tight to the van's backside. Through the rear window, Bob's little Jack Russell, Nancy, could be seen staring irritably at him.

Bob Gloster's van had always been a welcome sight in the past, but right now William wished mercilessly it didn't exist. Thankfully, as William needed to turn left at the crossroads, the van turned right. William cornered so sharply that he clipped the grass curb, nearly sending him reeling off the bike altogether. He was so focused on his direction and obscured by the van that he didn't notice his Uncle Rufus approaching the opposite way. Nor did he see Constable Stone pulling out from the right hand side to turn left up the hill, all using the crossroads simultaneously.

The distinctive rusty red bricks of the small housing estate that lay at the village's west side, soon appeared as William sped determinedly on. He pulled into the gravel drive, which was primarily used as a parking area since the houses were built on a steep slope and stone steps were necessary to reach the semi-terraced homes. The Pink's lived at number three, just two doors up from Tommy Andrews. William knocked expectantly on the door but there was no answer. He tried again with the same result. That's strange, he thought, and dashed round the front to look through the window. Within an open-plan living room he thought he saw someone duck hastily to the ground. Was Alphonza playing birthday games? He returned to the side door and peered through the letterbox.

'Alphonza... I know you're there,' he teased through the slit. He stood back and through the thick bubble glass could see the undeterminable shape of a figure looming towards him. The door opened and the figure stepped mysteriously back behind it. William sensed caution and peered apprehensively inside but before he could react, a praying mantis-like hand snatched his forearm and aggressively pulled him in. William felt the shock of a foot kicking him in the back, sending him crashing into the opposite wall. He spun round to glimpse his aggressor and was appalled to stare directly into the sly face of Troy Cruickshank.

'I might've known you'd be snooping round here Phillips,' he snapped, and reaching into the pocket of his denim jacket, pulled out a gun. 'Oh, by the way... Nice little museum of monsters you have there, Phillips. I was much impressed.' He nudged the head of the gun towards the kitchen. 'Over by the girl, now.'

William without question complied. Alphonza was huddled up in the corner, petrified.

'Alphonza,' he said, voice atremble. 'Tell me you're all right?'

Alphonza nodded, her hand grabbing William's. Their eyes fixed intently on Cruickshank. Upon the kitchen table before them stood a wolf pup.

'Nice little trophy,' remarked Cruickshank sarcastically, as he slipped some gum into his mouth. 'Funny that Miss Pike's house ain't it? People been swarming there like bee's to a honey pot...sweet meat.' He dragged a chair from beneath the table, rested his foot upon the seat and leant his elbow on his knee pointing the gun menacingly at Alphonza.

'I've been watching that house I have. Seen you I did, little girly, climbing out the window last Tuesday night…stealing the wolf you was. Now mama's out the way, little girly shows me where she put it, she did. Good little girly.'

They then heard a thud as the side door was pushed open. Cruickshank slipped the gun into his breast pocket and drew back to see who was at the door.

'Looks like the big boss has arrived at last,' he grinned, as a shadow from the passage entered the room. William and Alphonza stopped in shock at the sight of the cold eyes that then fastened upon them. Marcus Price stood quite composed in the small kitchen area looking at the two captives before him. His eyes then dropped coolly to the object on the table.

'Excellent, Cruickshank… You have done well,' said Price, as his hand reached out to grasp it. 'Your efforts will be rewarded.'

He placed a large black leather case on the table. Finding a key within his pocket he unfastened the locks, each of the brass clasps springing noisily from their sockets.

Price lifted the upper part of the case and taking the small pup packed it neatly inside. William leaned his head to see. Price noticing, swung the case teasingly round and tilted it towards him. William's heart sank. There, resting inside, were the six wolves.

'Observe, William Phillips, the wolves are mine once again,' he said with a smile, whilst staring deep into William's eyes. 'I can see you have discovered me… My mother saw it in my father, my former self, and through spite crushed him. A foolish move, for it was before the twins' birth. My soul was therefore able to linger and await the arrival of my present form, a form that contained, through blood, a determined strength. A strength that with knowledge grows stronger in each new earthbound life. And now destiny has brought these sacred carvings to me at a time that shows me great favour. Oh, if only you knew the wealth…the power that awaits me. However, time is money and I've not a moment to squander.' He turned the case back towards himself and drew the lid down. He then lifted it from the table and placed it by his side.

There was a ruthless dexterity about Price that was terrifying when, without words, he reached into his breast pocket and pulled out what looked like an old pendant. Holding it at arms length he allowed it to swing left to right. He fixed his eyes upon the two youngsters and began to recite some strange, unknown language.

'*Labora labora qeel sa estra aka runa... labora labora qeel sa estra aka runa*'

Spellbound, they watched its momentous golden glow as it hypnotically swung, left, right, left, right. Lulled by the language of the chant, their bodies relaxed.

'*Labora labora qeel sa estra aka runa.*'

Though quite transfixed by what he was witnessing, Cruickshank withdrew warily. Price continued to allow the pendant to swing and when fully satisfied, allowed it to gradually come to a halt. Calmly, he slipped the pendant back into the pocket of his immaculate tailored suit.

William and Alphonza stared mindlessly ahead. Hypnotised, they were now under the ownership of Price.

'I have your money, Mr Cruickshank, and perhaps a bonus for your efforts.' He picked up the case. 'Come with me, I have something I would like to show you. Oh, and bring the children... They are evidence that must be destroyed.'

Cruickshank looked at the two youngsters. 'I hope this bonus meets with my satisfaction,' he probed.

'Oh, it will Mr Cruikshank, I can assure you of that.' He gestured for Cruickshank to leave first, then motioned the children to follow. 'This way... That's it, that's it.'

They all departed the Pink's house and filed down to the bottom of the steep steps where Price's Range Rover was parked. As the two captives were seated in the rear, Bob Gloucester's ice-cream van could be heard piping away in the distance. Cruickshank spat out his gum and climbed eagerly into the front, whilst Price took the

wheel and gently pulled away, travelling east towards Great
Cheriton Wood.

Chapter 22

The Final Truth

The atmosphere in the Range Rover was extremely tense, made more so by Cruickshank, who found Price's collected calm unnerving. He hunched himself up against the passenger door ready for a quick escape, should he deem it necessary, and while peering through the windscreen to determine their direction, stole quick glances at Price to reassure himself of his own safety.

As the vehicle passed through Cheriton village, little did the residents know - some of whom were lost happily in their summer afternoon sleepy siesta's - of the impending doom that Price was about to unravel on their ill-prepared world.

Having made Cruickshank get out to open various gates, Price eventually drew up beside the mossy gate at the woodland's edge. He immediately disembarked, fervently clutching the black case, whilst ordering Cruickshank to leave the vehicle and release the two children from the rear.

'Follow me,' he clipped, as William and Alphonza, still caught in his spell, complied.

Price took the lead as he guided his company efficiently through the gate. As they entered the thick of the wood, the shady patterns of light flecking across their faces soon vanished.

'What's this, Price?' asked a wary Cruickshank. 'Teddy bear's picnic? Look, when do I get the readies?'

'Everything comes to he who waits...' returned Price, then under his breath, '...and I've waited long enough.'

They stretched on through the unwavering forest until Price reached its cloistered mysterious core. It had only been a few days since William had last visited this area of his haven, but now, under the dictatorship of Price, he was blinded to its familiarity.

They moved through the receding trees and pushed through prehistoric-looking tall ferns to reach the clearing at its heart. Price climbed the small mound before William's beloved old oak and rested his case within a cluster of bracken beneath its shadow of towering branches. His hands guided the two youngsters to one side and signalled them to halt. Cruickshank was growing restless.

'I've had enough, Price… Let's do away with the kids and go.'

'Hold!' commanded Price. 'Prepare yourself for a life-force more powerful than you could ever imagine.'

Price selected William with a transfixed stare. He raised his hand and with a hard dry click of his fingers released him from his hypnotic state. William, blinking wildly, stumbled back catching his breath as he came to.

'Welcome, William, to the alter of my kingdom.' Price watched him gather his bearings with a dominant glare. 'It's been a long time, a very long time indeed. I smelt your presence long before the fete. I just couldn't believe that Nature should rest her future in the hands of a child. As all have witnessed, William, over the last one hundred years, the dark material forces of this world are taking their rightful hold. I speak in the voice of humans in your time when I say economy before nature for that is the true destiny we must follow. You could have had a slice of my realm, William. Its cost was not yours to mourn, but like a poor simple fool you have chosen to bemoan your fate. The richness of this wood is well past its prime. Its harvest shall be part of the new growth for all to share. Its death is unimportant in this independent age.'

'In this age of greed you mean,' returned a fully responsive William. 'Independence is freedom, not a right to take while others suffer at your cost, the cost of your greed. Life is not a competition…it's what it is… life. And the life of this wood and all those who care about its existence have no say against your necessity for greed. You manipulate people with the fear that they shall lose out, be left behind. You do this simply by raising the stakes, by raising the price, your price…and as that travels up, so does everything else with it, including crime!' William's shoulders fell back amazed by his own defence, a defence from his own higher self. Price laughed.

'You're too late, William Phillips, as an ambassador of your kind, you are too late.'

'No, I'm here and that's enough,' announced William. 'Nature, like history, takes her revenge on those who choose to ignore her. She can deny you, but not you her! You've come back time and time again and still you haven't learned. I feel sorry for you, Price. You fail to develop because you're too scared to face the truth - your ego won't permit it.'

Price ignored him and turned to face the centre of the clearing below the old oak. With a deep breath he then raised his chest, his heavily lashed eyelids relaxing as he cast his arms out reverently to the centre of the wood. The black arts that he had so long practised over the centuries would be now put to their ultimate effect.

'*Respleneth fortuta ironcoth beholdin... Respleneth fortuta ironcoth beholdin.*'

Suddenly, the loose dead leaves on the ground before Price began to lift and stir, swirling round in a clockwise motion.

'*Respleneth fortuta ironcoth beholdin.*'

Price's face grew intense as the leaves started to gather momentum, lifting higher and spinning relentlessly from the ground, creating a cyclonic effect that widened the circle further. Heavy clouds began to gather in the sky, placing a darkened veil over those below. Sparkling reams of light began to flash amid the sweep of leaves. William watched in amazement as high above, shots of lightning forked down into the epicentre of the building leafy whirlpool. Magically, amidst the leaves, water began to emerge, whirling and swirling into an immense pool that grumbled menacingly.

Still in a deep trance, Alphonza stood motionless, whilst Cruikshank looking on guardedly, watched Price draw the waters up before him.

Finally, in all its enormous glory, the whirlpool's deep gaping mouth emerged, glistening and gurgling, its tremendous chasm dropping deep beyond eyesight's reach. Price turned to face his audience.

'You see, William, denial turns to hate and hate turns to power. I shall be rewarded.' Turning to Cruickshank, he pulled a bundle of notes from his breast pocket. 'I believe this belongs to you, Mr Cruickshank.'

A watchful Cruickshank moved towards Price, stopping at a safe distance from him and the whirlpool.

'You want your bonus?' said Price. 'Well, come and get it.'

For a moment Cruickshank held back, then placed his hand within his breast pocket and retrieved the gun.

'I'll take more than the money, Price, and you'd better do as I say or you'll find a bullet in your head.' He pointed the gun at Price. 'Hand me the wolves, now.'

Price made no effort to reach for the case. Instead he moved towards Cruickshank.

'Step any closer and I'll blow your brains out,' warned Cruickshank.

Price continued to make towards him.

'Stop now!'

Three shots rang out.

No blood appeared from Price's head, not a drop, for the very summoning of the whirlpool had shrouded him in a cloak of protective power.

Cruickshank fired three more shots at point-blank range, but to no avail. And before he had time to retreat, Price grabbed his arm, squeezing his wrist so tightly the gun loosened immediately from his grasp, dropping into the tufts of bracken below. Cruickshank fought like a wild animal but was soon overwhelmed by the figure of Price, who had wrapped his arms around him like a serpent, smothering his kicks and punches. Then with undeniable strength, Price's large hands grasped Cruickshank around his haunch and neck, lifting his struggling body high above him.

'No!' screamed Cruickshank, but it was too late. With a roar, Price wrenched the violent body from his grasp and tossed it into the centre of the whirlpool's mouth. They all watched in horror, the flailing form of Cruikshank vanish into the abyss.

Price turned to William.

'You see, Nature takes no prisoners. She is not forgiving.' Amid all the chaos Price had not spoken a truer word.

'All the more reason to respect her, then!' exclaimed a very concerned William.

Price grinned. 'You needn't look so worried, William Phillips. Criuckshank's amongst good company - the lovely Livia, miserly Huntly Roach, my dear sister, Judith, and my most blessed of mothers, the fair Miss Pike - they're all down there. You see, William, I like my conscience clean!' Price gave a guttural laugh. 'And now for the girl.' He motioned his hand to call her forth.

'No, Alphonza, no!' William leapt before her and shook her wildly. Price drew out his arm and Alphonza imitated his action, pushing William to the ground with remarkable strength. Undeterred, Alphonza walked obediently towards the pool.

Lifting himself from the ground, William charged at Price who grasped and held out his fighting adversary with a single hand. Alphonza drew nearer to the immense current. Within a step, she would be plunging its depths.

'Stop!' yelled a faint yet authoritative voice from the dimness of the wood.

William and Price turned to see a uniformed figure wrestling amid the ferns, heading towards them. It wasn't long before a flush-faced Constable Stone became visible. Price's eyes fixed on him with mock sympathy.

'Is something wrong, Constable?' he patronised. 'You look a little red in the face.'

Although startled and shocked by the scene before him, Constable Stone, seeing a helpless William swinging from Price's grasp, soon mustered courage and approached him.

'Marcus Price, I don't know what game you think you are playing here but you can release that boy now!'

Price, unflinching, just stared at the Constable.

'Did you hear me Price?

Price said nothing.

'Now come on Price, it has been brought to my attention that you have something to do with these people going missing. Now, if you would just release William and allow me to escort you to the police station to answer a few questions…let's not make things difficult!'

Price threw William to the ground and marched coldly towards his diversion. Constable Stone braced his arms for a tackle.

'Now I won't tell you again Price!'

Price loomed over the Constable and positioned his fist in line with the Constable's head.

'Now Price, don't be trouble!'

Like a pneumatic riveter, Price's hand punched, knocking the Constable out cold.

'There goes your insurance, William…Tut tut!'

'What makes you think there aren't others on their way,' warned William. 'Lost in your own power you forgot yourself. Time's no longer on your side, Price, and I have the bounty!' He pulled back some ferns to reveal the black case.

'And I have the girl.' Price again motioned Alphonza to move.

'Right!' began William. 'I know these woods like the back of my hand, if I run you will never find me.'

For a moment Price stared hard at William and cautioned his thoughts.

'Let's make a bargain then,' he resolved, 'the girl's life for the wolves'.'

William drew courage and held out the case. 'Deal.'

Price snapped his fingers at Alphonza, who recoiled to the ground. William ran to her aid, as Price groped for the case. Retrieving it he hauled it towards the water's edge and as fast as he could, sprang open the locks exposing the contents. He unravelled the black cloth that covered them, drew out the first of the pups and held it up.

'Mark William, mark!' he hailed as he threw the first of the carvings into the beckoning waters. He gathered the second and hurled that in too, then ceremoniously continued with the others until only the parents remained. Taking a gratified glance at William, he stood up and with relish threw in the final two carvings. He stepped back expectantly, William and a much-confused Alphonza allowing him a wide birth.

For a while nothing happened. All three of them stared with bated breath, awaiting some form of reaction from the swirling expanse. Price's eyes flashed across at William. Then the light about them began to fade even darker, rasps of lightening again shot down into the whirlpool's throat followed by sharp cracks of thunder. Confused and terrified, Alphonza held herself around William. The blinding flashes began to grow so intense that the spectators had to shield their eyes. Suddenly, from the heart of the pool an oval beam of light shot up and hovered over its axis. Price's eyes widened and with an arm out-stretched he moved towards it, the stupendous oval light remaining still. Then slowly, as if beguiled by some magnetic force, it started to move towards him. Price's hand reached out over the water, his fingers splaying like hooks. The two youngsters stared in pure wonder. The bright light was now well within Price's grasp and he bathed his hand within its glow to draw out a magnificent shimmering key. A tear rolled down his cheek and he laughed with unbridled relief, holding the key tightly to his breast.

'You see, William, the legacy of the six wolves has not come to pass. With the possession of this key the spirit of nature's keepers shall remain forever buried and with it, you and your kind's hope. Without hope your strength will diminish and die. I shall now close the circle of water.'

Price turned and raised his arms high.

'*Inz stefaneez frobreezay confronti cloz...*' Suddenly, a piece of turf hit Price's head, sprinkling soil all over his shoulder. Startled, he swung round to catch its perpetrator but the woods behind him lay still. He stared coldly at William who with Alphonza, was also glancing round for the deliverer. Undeterred, Price marched back to the pool to conclude his ceremony. '*Clozreth nedforam inz...*' again he stopped, for staring at him from across the waters was a young girl.

'Not going to take the crock of gold all for yourself, are you Price?' Leigh was calmly holding her own. 'I might be a child, but I have a tongue and I can certainly use it!'

'And I have the key,' he retorted with glee, holding it up triumphantly. 'That will make my domination absolute. Opposition is pointless!'

Price then gave a sudden resonant groan as an enormous branch plummeted and cracked across his unsuspecting back. The blow sent the key spinning and spinning high into the air. Everyone watched in awe as it eventually began to fall back towards the whirlpool.

'No!' yelled Price, his face paling in horror. But just as it looked as if the key was going to drop below the raging surface, it spun back up. It had become caught in the thin, spiralling, branches of the old oak. Price turned sharply round to see Rufus clutching the remains of the torn branch, but his invasion held no interest to him. Instead he scrambled to the base of the tree and began to climb the trunk. Leigh immediately ran round to comfort Alphonza, whilst William and Rufus headed towards the tree.

'Get down man!' shouted Rufus. 'You're walking a tight-rope to death!'

But Price had his attention only on the key and with manic desperation continued to clamber through the thick branches. The key flickered, its golden sparkles entrancing Price to climb higher to reach it. The distance between Price and the key diminished. Eagerly, he stepped onto a sturdy branch and began to edge his way closer and closer towards the key, his hands clutching the upper branches for support. He was nearly there, but as he stretched out his arm to snatch the emblem of his future, an almighty crack reverberated beneath his feet and the branch began to give way. A desperate Price grabbed at the branch above.

'Hold on!' shouted William, racing towards the base of the tree and hauling himself up after Price.

'Get down, William, you fool! You'll be killed!' screamed Rufus, as he clutched the trunk.

In a matter of seconds William reached the struggling Price. Pulling himself over a branch, he leaned out to reach him.

'Help me, please...I *beg* you!' cried Price, his face stricken with fear. The magnitude of the pool seemed to suddenly drain the man of his exalted power.

William offered his hand.

'Hold on to me and swing over...you can do it!' Price's trembling arm thrashed out like a fisherman's rod, his fingers barely touching William's.

'Again!' shouted William.

Sweat poured from Price's brow. Out swung his flailing arm. Their hands knotted, their eyes met. Within all the intensity, William saw a human, whose ego had fallen, providing Price with the opportunity to experience a less shackled life. The vulnerable man was now held still, within moments he would be hauled to safety. But the upper branch that Price held began to splinter. The girls screamed hysterically, as Rufus began to clamber up the tree.

'Help me please... Oh, no...Please!' wailed Price. But it was no use. The branch only split further until hanging by mere threads, dipping Price's feet into the water.

'Oh, Gods...' he cried out, staring desperately at William. 'Forgive me...forgive me!'

William looked at Price with horror and shock. The man's greed had turned in on itself, revealing a face to be pitied. With a final tear, the branch splintered from the trunk. Price's body dropped, vanishing finally into depths below.

The others watched, stricken, as suddenly he reappeared, splashing and gasping for air. Like some great beast before the kill, the whirlpool tossed and teased him, spinning him helplessly around, each circle drawing him nearer and nearer toward its hungry mouth. Helpless, there was nothing anyone could do except stare as the pitiful figure fought vainly against the current. With a final pleading cry, the waters engulfed him.

The witnesses to the event slunk back appalled. And then there was a truly almighty, rumble…thud…crack.

'Oh, no,' breathed William. Not my tree!' He clutched himself around a branch - the old oak was collapsing.

'Get down now, William…quick!' implored Rufus, as the huge belly of the tree started to lean. All those on land were screaming as they groped around the base. William, like a monkey, started to descend. He was nearing the bottom when his foot slipped and he found himself dangling above the snatching waters. Leigh pulled at her hair. Another almighty crack came from the base.

'Swing out, William,' yelled Rufus. 'Swing out!' As the girls clung to his waist, trying desperately to anchor him, he leant out over the water.

'One, two, three,' shouted William, as he swung towards Rufus. Rufus frantically clutched at William's legs, just as the branch finally snapped and broke away. William's body plunged into the indifferent current, but Rufus's arms tightened their grip, holding fast. Pulling with all their strength, Leigh and Alphonza and Rufus, all dragged a soaked coughing William from the water. But all was not over yet. With a deep, earthy tremble, the great oak began to collapse into the whirlpool.

'The key,' said William, pointing.

Transfixed, they watched as the long veined branch that held the emblem of fate descended towards the water's centre. Like a hand, its frail twig-like fingers opened out as if delivering its treasure back from whence it came. Gravity then took hold and the key dropped finally from its rest, returning to the depths below. With a final wrenching tear the aged oak started its descent, its canopy of branches crashing into the water.

'Get back everyone!' demanded Rufus, as its gigantic roots tore themselves from their sleep, whip-lashing high into the air. The sound was deafening as its immense body started to break into the water.

'We've got to get out of here, now,' shouted Rufus, as he and the girls began to distance themselves from the terrifying scene.

Noticing that William was not heeding his words, Rufus ran back to gather him.

'William, I don't know what's been unearthed here,' he said, clutching the youngster's arm, 'but it's very dangerous. We have to get out…fast!'

'I can't leave!' pleaded William, as he pulled away from him.

'Come on, William!' screamed Leigh, backing her uncle. 'This is madness!'

The great oak had been torn fully from its woodland throne, its huge body now tipping completely upside down. The main body drifted into the centre, its roots spiralling high into the air. Here it seemed to pause, restive for a few moments before, with a rumble, beginning to sink. Water jetted from air-locked holes as deeper and deeper it sank until its trembling remnants could be seen no more.

The woods around them lit up with lightening followed by a resounding clap of thunder that shook the very heart of the wood.

'Come on, William!' insisted Rufus, again with gritted teeth.

'No!' he replied, rooting himself to the spot. 'I'm staying. I want to see the truth!'

Abandoning their attempt to escape, the two girls ran back to join Rufus and William who remained a clear distance from the waters. Petrified, they all huddled together, staring intently into the pool as a gathering wind smacked around them.

Suddenly they noticed a change in the whirlpool - the current seemed to be altering direction. It was hard to determine if it was a halting or reversal effect. The sky above them rumbled on. Bewildered they watched as one current fought against another, the clockwise motion becoming less and less evident as the anti-clockwise motion seemed to unlock the water's pattern, pushing the current back.

Gradually the mouth of the whirlpool began to disappear altogether until it was reduced to a tiny eye. Finally, with a crack of thunder it vanished, delivering the waters into one great mass. Terrified, they crouched down to watch as the pool's middle now splashed high into the air. With an enormous gush the drawn up wave collapsed outward from its centre, sending a rush of water into the surrounding banks. A silence followed.

The four figures straightened up and peered about themselves. The wood fell eerily still. With a startling flutter, a bird sprang from the undergrowth beyond. It was then that a wraithlike mist began to form on the calm, leaf-flaked surface of the water.

From a long way down, deep within the depths of the pool, a pale blue light could be seen emerging, glowing brighter and brighter as it began to reach the water's surface. The observers stepped back as the strange light began to break through the pool's face. Everyone drew a breath of trepidation as the light began to form a shape. Slowly the features of a small animal started to appear - legs, neck, head, nose and frightened eyes becoming visible. William and his friends stood awestruck. Before them, emerging from its prison of hundreds of years was a fully formed wolf pup. There it stood, glowing wondrously on the waters edge.

They all marvelled at the first of the released pups, its soft, vulnerable features trembling, its timid, soulful eyes searching for bearings. Behind it another cusp of light broke, then another and another, until all four of the tiny young pups emerged. The confused creatures huddled together and stared at the four humans. The first of the pups, gaining a little confidence with the arrival of its brothers and sisters, started to peer more questioningly at those before him. The pup to his left, a small female, looked proud while the female to his right was startled and apprehensive. Huddled between them was the youngest of the creatures, a tiny male, fragile and wary.

'Beautiful,' whispered Alphonza. 'They're beautiful.'

A light breeze caressed the trees, then a huge ball of light emerged from behind the pups, the mother wolf in all her glory had surfaced. Rufus and the youngsters stepped back as an even more awesome mountain of light sprang from the depths. The magnificent male had lurched from his rest and joined his family. Gathering them behind him, he fixed his eyes upon the creatures ahead.

'Everyone remain calm,' breathed William. 'There're just as frightened as we are. We mustn't appear to be a threat.'

'Maybe we should take to our heels,' suggested Rufus wryly. 'That's the least threatening action.'

'No,' replied William. 'That would show fear, they wouldn't trust that.'

The wolf pack drew together, their mystical glow radiating outwards. The male wolf then looked up and stared intently at William before lowering his head and starting toward him. Leigh tried to take her brother's arm as everyone bar him stepped back, but William remained calm and faced the glaring animal.

'William are you crazy?' whispered Rufus, halting his retreat to watch his vulnerable nephew. William didn't look back to catch their withdrawal, instead he took a deep breath and stepped towards the bristling animal.

Allowing himself a safe distance he knelt down. The wolf's eyes followed him with questioning interest. William returned the fascination, each studying the other deeply. William smiled and the wolf, pricking up his ears, tilted his head, his almond eyes peering at him with a warm, affectionate curiosity. William reached out his hand and the wolf stepped nobly towards it, allowing William to caress his soft silver cheek. Like brothers united, they expressed respectful acceptance. William felt his body tingle with an enlightened knowledge of wisdom that he and the animal shared, a deep held belief, an inseparable love for nature, for all things pure.

Contented, the wolf stepped back and breaking from the union, ran to the mound on which the old oak once stood. Here he looked at his pack whose eyes had studied him. Then, as if recognising a silent understanding, the pups, in turn, followed their mother and joined him. The male wolf then turned back for a final glance at William, who rose happily to his feet, his watery eyes saying goodbye.

The wolf looked out across the woods ahead and dropping from the mound he and the mother led their family away, pacing lightly across the water's still surface that seemed to recede with each delicate step. Their bodies glowed blue-white as they travelled into the distance, until their ghostly spirits disappeared into the density of the woods beyond.

Alphonza, Rufus, Leigh and William stood speechless, unable to find words to convey their feelings. Finally, a shaken Rufus broke their silence and walked towards his sister's son. He placed an arm around his shoulder.

'I have no understanding of what I've just experienced,' he trembled, 'but of one thing I can be sure, you are a very brave young man, William.'

'No,' he replied. 'I just trusted my instinct that's all, and I had the good fortune of kind people to guide me.'

Their attention was soon taken by a rustling noise a short distance away - a semi-conscious Constable Stone was wining madly, his poor right eye being redder than his famous cheeks.

'Price,' he yelled. 'Don't let him get away.'

Rufus and the two girls rushed to his aid, leaving William a moment of solace to reflect upon all that had passed before him. He looked out to where the wolves had journeyed and could see a faint green figure standing resolute between the trees. William watched as the Mysterious Man raised his hand in a thoughtful salute. Then, as he had always done, he simply disappeared.

EPILOGUE

Cheriton village lay in a small shallow, a few miles from the busy throb of a dual carriageway from which veined various roads that encircled its breadth. Cheriton was a village that you could easily pass, its charm unseen.

The narrow road that meandered through it witnessed a pleasing array of homes, some large, some small, some cloaked in creepers, whilst others nestled beneath the shade of aged trees. All in turn provided a home for an assortment of busy creatures that help make up the gamut of life.

From a hovering kestrel's eye you could see its ornate leafy heart, spreading from which were the church, manor, hall, shop and the old school. To the north lay a small housing estate, to the west, fields. A weary farm lay in the south, while in the east stretched a rich, dense, ancient wood.

As does everything, Cheriton and its 'life' was changing. Although some carried on regardless of the world's activities, others gave time to pause for necessary thought.

The season was summer and as the sun's bright rays began to drop to early evening, the gold, parched, cut grass of Cheriton's fields glistened from its recent harvest.

A dishevelled Land Rover could be seen passing through an open gate, pulling up near a hedge where stood an old motorbike. Three adults, an elderly lady and a small black-and-white dog, climbed from the vehicle.

Across the way a party of five people could be seen emerging from the outskirts of a wood, their faces wearing expressions of shock, horror, confusion and exhilaration.

Directly behind them something else emerged from the shadowy veil, something that couldn't be seen but perhaps felt - it was an energy, an energy called hope...hope for a more conscious mankind.

The real adventure was just beginning.

About the author

Alan Calder Rawlings was raised on a farm in Somerset where he worked as a dairyman and gardener before moving to London to study drama for three years. In between a variety of jobs, he has toured both England and Europe as an actor in leading and supporting roles.

The Legacy of the Six Wolves is his first work of fiction. He currently lives in the West Country where he is working on a new trilogy of books which he intends to release in the near future.

For comments and further information email: rawearth22@btinternet.com